PEACE TALES

EMANUEL PERDIS
DIRECTOR
Tel: + 61 2 8306 9099
Mob: + 61 41 2288 081

Humans are warring creatures.
They will fight to defend their land and possessions.
They will fight for the right to do as they please.

Humans will also fight to take land or possessions
from others.
They will fight to control the actions and thoughts
of other humans.

For humans peace does not come easily.
They must work hard at compromising with others
to make peace happen.
The first step on the path to peace is choosing peace.

This book will help you think about peace as a choice.
Perhaps you will choose peace.
Perhaps not.

P E A C E
T A L E S

WORLD FOLKTALES TO TALK ABOUT

By Margaret Read MacDonald

LINNET BOOKS   1992

© 1992 Margaret Read MacDonald.
All rights reserved. First published 1992 by Linnet Books,
an imprint of The Shoe String Press, Inc.
North Haven, Connecticut 06473

Permissions are included in the Acknowledgments
following the text.

Library of Congress Cataloging-in-Publication Data

Peace tales : world folktales to talk about /
[compiled] by Margaret Read MacDonald.
p.   cm.
Includes bibliographical references and index.
Summary: A collection of folktales
from cultures around the world, reflecting
different aspects of war and peace.
1. Tales [1. Folklore. 2. War—Folklore. 3. Peace—Folklore.]
I. MacDonald, Margaret Read, 1940–
PZ8.1.P3145 1992   92-8994   398.2—dc20
ISBN 0-208-02328-3 (cloth : alk. paper) : $22.50
ISBN 0-208-02329-1 (paper : alk. paper) : $13.95

Printed in the United States of America

The paper in this publication meets the
minimum requirements of the American National
Standard for Information Sciences—Permanence
of Paper for Printed Library Materials,
ANSI Z39.48–1984. ⊗

Designed by Abigail Johnston in Friz Quadrata
display and Bookman Light text.

Illustrated by Zobra Anasazi.

To the memory of Floating Eagle Feather,
who traveled the world sowing stories
in the hopes of making this a better planet.
He has passed on, but the world's need for stories
of love, peace, and ecological caring . . . remains.

ॐ

In the joy of story,
in the power of story,
to create a world of power and joy
for all living beings.
—FLOATING EAGLE FEATHER'S CREDO

CONTENTS

*An asterisk marks those titles
specially formatted by Margaret
Read MacDonald for retelling.

2 ❧ PEACE

PATHWAYS TO PEACE ❧

PEACEMAKING TECHNIQUES ❧

PEACEMAKERS ❧

STEPS TO PEACE

Step 1. Choose peace.

Step 2. Try to understand the needs
of the other humans on this planet.

Step 3. Learn to compromise with those others.

Step 4. Work constantly to improve your understanding
and your compromises.

Peace is possible.
But it must be chosen.

PEACE
TALES

CHOICES

PROLOGUE

The Gates
of Paradise ❧

A soldier named Nobushige came to Hakuin, and asked: "Is there really a paradise and a hell?"

"Who are you?" inquired Hakuin.

"I am a samurai," the warrior replied.

"You, a soldier!" exclaimed Hakuin. "What kind of ruler would have you as his guard? Your face looks like that of a beggar."

Nobushige became so angry that he began to draw his sword, but Hakuin continued: "So you have a sword! Your weapon is probably much too dull to cut off my head."

As Nobushige drew his sword Hakuin remarked: "Here open the gates of hell!"

At these words the samurai, perceiving the master's discipline, sheathed his sword and bowed.

"Here open the gates of paradise," said Hakuin.

—A ZEN TALE

1

PATHWAYS
TO WAR

STUBBORNNESS

Two Goats
on the Bridge ❧

Between two mountains lay a narrow bridge.
On each mountain lived a goat.
Some days the goat from the western mountain would
cross the bridge to graze on the eastern mountain.
Some days the goat from the eastern mountain would
cross the bridge to graze on the western mountain.
But one day both goats began to cross the bridge
at the same time.

Those goats met in the middle of the bridge.
Neither wanted to give way.
"Move off!" shouted the Western Goat.
"*I* am crossing this bridge."

"Move yourself!" bawled the Eastern Goat.
"*I* am crossing here!"

As neither would retreat and neither could move forward,
they stood in anger for some time.

Then at last they locked horns and began to push.
They were so evenly matched in strength that they succeeded
only in pushing *each other* off the bridge.
Wet and furious they climbed from the river and stomped off to
their homes.
Each could be heard to mutter,
"See what *his* stubbornness caused."

—A TALE FROM RUSSIA

Chiang chung sui ta,
Ch-uan i yu hsiang chuang.

Although the river is broad,
there are times when boats collide.

—A CHINESE PROVERB

SUSPICION

The Neighbor's Shifty Son ෨

A farmer once lost his axe.
He felt certain that his neighbor had stolen the axe.
He watched that neighbor with suspicion.
He noticed that the neighbor's son seemed as shifty
as his father.
That boy looked just like a thief.
The farmer knew he could not trust either of them.

One day when he visited a distant field where he sometimes
worked, the farmer discovered his axe.
He had left it behind the last time he worked in that field.

When the farmer returned home he noticed his
neighbor's son at play.
The boy looked absolutely normal now.
There seemed nothing shifty or suspicious about him at all.

—A TALE FROM CHINA

Lembu bertandok panjang,
tiada manadok pun,
di-kata orang ia menandok juga.

An ox with long horns,
even if he does not butt,
will be accused of butting.

—A MALAY PROVERB

A Dervish Hosts the Mullah ❧

It is said that the Mullah Nasrudin once took shelter in a Dervish's cave. The Mullah had been wandering lost for a long while and was quite thirsty. Now that night had fallen he huddled in the Dervish's cave, quite terrified.

After a while the Mullah asked the Dervish for water.

"I have none in the cave," said the Dervish. "But go down to the spring. It is not far."

The Mullah was much too frightened to venture out into the dark night alone, even for a drink of water.

"Well, then I will go and bring you water," said the Dervish at last.

"No! Don't go out and leave me *alone* in this dark cave!"

"Here is a knife," said the Dervish. "If something attacks you can defend yourself with it. But really, you will be quite safe here."

While the Dervish was gone, the Mullah began to imagine all sorts of evils which might enter the cave and attack him. When the Dervish returned with the water, the Mullah shouted in horror and began to stab the air with a sword.

"Halt!" screamed the Mullah.

"But it is only I, the Dervish. I have returned with your water."

"That is what you *say*. You could be any sort of demon!" And the Mullah continued to defend himself against his imagined horrors.

"This is only *fear*," said the Dervish. "It is causing you damage."

"I agree," said the Mullah. "But once you *catch* fear, you *have* it. And the bad thing is, you don't even have to *have* it yourself to suffer from it!"

"So I see," said the Dervish. And he went in search of another place to spend the night.

—A SUFI TALE

꙳

Im Kreige schweight das Recht.

In war, justice is silent.

—A GERMAN PROVERB

Reaching for the Moon ❧

One night the King of the Monkeys noticed a glorious
golden moon lying at the bottom of a pool.
Not realizing that this was but a reflection,
the King called on his subjects to come at once and haul up the
treasure trove of gold.
"Our strongest monkey shall hold onto this tree," said the King.
"And our second strongest monkey shall hold onto *his* hand,
reach into the water, and fetch up the golden moon."
They tried this.
But the second monkey could not reach the moon.

"Who is our third strongest monkey?
Come hold onto your brother's hand and reach into the
water for that moon."
But still the moon was out of reach.

"Bring up the fourth strongest monkey.
Let him climb down and try."
Now those monkeys were hanging in a chain, each dangling
from the arms of the other.
The fourth monkey climbed down the chain and hung from the

hand of the third monkey . . . but still the moon was out of
    reach.
And so they continued . . . five . . . six . . . seven . . . eight . . .
monkey after monkey added to the chain until they touched
        the water's surface.

"We are almost touching it!" called up the monkeys.
"Then let me be the first to hold it!" cried the King,
and he scurried down the chain to the very bottom.

But the weight of all this foolishness had become too
        much for the strongest monkey
        who was still holding to the tree at the top.
Just as the King reached into the water for his moon
that strongest monkey lost his grasp.
So those monkeys fell, every one of them, into the deep pool.
There they drowned, along with their King.

He who follows an unwise leader, is himself a fool.
                              —A TALE FROM TIBET

*Miekka tappaa yhden,
mutta kieli tappaa tuhansia.*

A sword kills one,
but a tongue kills thousands.
                —A FINNISH PROVERB

Strength 🦎

The animals decided to have a contest
to see who was the strongest.
This contest was Elephant's idea.
"Everybody meet on Wednesday.
We'll see who has STRENGTH."

First to arrive was Chimpanzee.
Chimpanzee came in jumping around.
   "Strength!
    I've got strength.
    See these ARMS!
    Just wait till they see my strength!"
Chimpanzee sat down.

Deer arrived.
   "Strength!
    Look at these LEGS!
    I have SUCH strength."
Deer sat down.

Next came Leopard.
Leopard was showing his claws and growling.
   "Strength!
    Look at these CLAWS!
    I . . . have STRENGTH!"
Leopard sat down.

In came Bushbuck.
Bushbuck lowered his strong horns.
   "Strength!
    See these horns!
    THIS is strength."
Bushbuck sat down.

Elephant came in.
Elephant moved so slowly.
    "El . . . e . . . phant . . .
    MEANS
    Strength."
Elephant sat down.

They waited.
They waited.
One more animal to come.
They waited.
At last Man came running in.
    "STRENGTH! STRENGTH!"
Man was showing off his muscles.
    "Here I am.
    We can START now!"

Man had brought his gun to the forest.
Man had been hiding his gun in the bush.
That is why he was late.
Elephant took charge.
    "Now that *Man* is finally here, we can begin.
    Chimpanzee.
    Show us strength."

Chimpanzee jumped up.
He ran to a small tree and climbed it.
He bent it over and tied it in a knot.
He climbed back down.
    "Strength! Was that strength?!!
    What strength!"

The animals cheered.
    "Strength! Strength! Strength! Strength!
    THAT's strength!"
The animals calmed down.
    "Well . . .

Chimpanzee
SIT DOWN.
Who is next?"

Deer leaped up.
Deer ran three miles into the forest.
Deer ran three miles back.
Deer wasn't even out of breath.
   "There.
    Wasn't that strength!

The animals agreed.
   "Strength! Strength! Strength! Strength!
    That was STRENGTH!"

   "Well . . .
    Deer
    SIT DOWN.
    Who's next?"

Leopard leaped up.
Leopard drew out his long claws.
He began to scrape at the earth.
    Scrung . . . scrung . . . scrung . . . scrung . . .
That dirt just flew!
The animals jumped back.
They were frightened.
   "Aaaah!
    Wasn't that strength?"

   "Strength! Strength! Strength! Strength!
    That was STRENGTH!"

   "Well . . .
    Leopard
    SIT DOWN.
    Who's next?"

Elephant fell over.
Dead.
Dead.

Man was jumping and bragging.
  "Strength! Strength!
   Wasn't THAT strength?!"

  "Strength. . . . "

Man looked around.
The animals were gone.
They had fled into the forest.
   "Strength! . . ."
There was no one left to hear him brag.
Man was alone.

In the forest the animals huddled together and talked.
   "Did you see that?"
   "Was that strength?"
   "Would you call that strength?"
   "No. That was DEATH."
   "That was DEATH."

Since that day the animals will not walk with Man.
When Man enters the forest he has to walk by himself.

The animals still talk of Man . . .
That creature *Man*. . . .
He is the one who cannot tell the difference
      between strength
      and death.
                    —A LIMBA TALE FROM WEST AFRICA

ઙ♪

Silah sahibine bile düṣmandir.

A weapon is an enemy even to its owner.
                    —A TURKISH PROVERB

Not Our Problem 🍃

The King sat with his Adviser eating honey on puffed rice.
As they ate they leaned from the palace window
and watched the street below.
They talked of this and that.
The King, not paying attention to what he was doing,
let a drop of honey fall onto the windowsill.
"Oh sire, let me wipe that up," offered the Adviser.
"Never mind," said the King.
"It is not *our* problem.
The servants will clean it later."

As the two continued to dine on their honey and puffed rice,
the drop of honey slowly began to drip down the windowsill.
At last it fell with a plop onto the street below.
Soon a fly had landed on the drop of honey and begun
his own meal.
Immediately a gecko sprang from under the palace and with a flip
of its long tongue swallowed the fly.
But a cat had seen the gecko and pounced.
Then a dog sprang forward and attacked the cat!

"Sire, there seems to be a cat and dog fight in the street.

    Should we call someone to stop it?"
"Never mind," said the King.

    "It's not *our* problem."
So the two continued to munch their honey and puffed rice.

Meanwhile the cat's owner had arrived and was beating the dog.
The dog's owner ran up and began to beat the cat.
Soon the two were beating each other.

"Sire, there are two *persons* fighting in the street now.

    Shouldn't we send someone to break this up?"
The King lazily looked from the window.
"Never mind.

    It's not *our* problem."

The friends of the cat's owner gathered and began to
        cheer him on.
The friends of the dog's owner began to cheer her on as well.
Soon both groups entered the fight and attacked each other.

"Sire, a number of people are fighting in the street now.

    Perhaps we should call someone to break this up."
The King was too lazy even to look.
You can guess what he said.
"Never mind.

    It's not *our* problem."

Now soldiers arrived on the scene.
At first they tried to break up the fighting.
But when they heard the cause of the fight
some sided with the cat's owner.
Others sided with the dog's owner.
Soon the soldiers too had joined the fight.

With the soldiers involved, the fight erupted into civil war.
Houses were burned down.
People were harmed.
And the palace itself was set afire and burned to the ground.
The King and his Adviser stood surveying the ruins.
"Perhaps," said the King,
   "I was wrong?
     Perhaps the drop of honey WAS our problem."

—A TALE FROM BURMA AND THAILAND

Yabu wo tsutsuite hebi wo dasu.

By poking at a bamboo thicket
you drive out a snake.

—A JAPANESE PROVERB

A Man with No Brain 🍂

I n the past, many things happened!
Many things happened in days gone by!
Basil and lily I offer to the Prophet Mohammed. May God bless and honor him!

Here is, among others, the adventure of the renowed Jouha. In Algeria he is called Jha, or else Ben Sakrane. Farther to the east, he is Nasredin Hodja. He is, in fact, Tyl Eulenspiegel, or Jean le Sot; the fool who sells his wisdom, he who brays like a donkey in order to be heard, and sometimes the most unbeatably cunning.

So, one day Jha met some friends armed for battle: shields, spears, bows, and quivers full of arrows.

"But where are you going in these disguises?"

"Listen, don't you know that we are professional soldiers? We are obviously going to take part in a battle, and it promises to be rough!"

"Good! This is my one chance to see what happens in these things that I've heard about but never seen with my own eyes. Let me go with you to see it, at least once!"

"Well, come then! You are welcome!"

And there he was among the small platoon which was going to the battlefield to join the rest of the army.

The first arrow planted itself in his forehead!

Quick! A surgeon! He arrived, examined the wounded man, nodded, and declared, "It has gone in deep! To remove it will be easy. But if the tiniest piece of brain is on it, he is lost!"

The wounded man seized the doctor's hand and kissed it, expressing his "deep gratitude to the Master," and declared, "Doctor, you can remove the arrow without fear; there won't be the tiniest atom of brain on it."

"You be quiet!" said the doctor. "And let the experts take care of you. How can you tell that it hasn't reached your brain?"

"I know only too well," said Jha, "because if I had the slightest particle of brains, I would never have come with my 'friends.' "

—A TALE FROM ALGERIA BY MOHAMMED BEL-HALFAOUI,
TRANSLATED BY CATHRYN WELLNER.

*El que no quiere ruido
que no crie cochinos.*

If you don't like noise,
don't raise pigs.

—A MEXICAN-AMERICAN
PROVERB

A WEAPON BEYOND CONTROL

The Weapon ॐ

There was a chief.
His relatives lived in five towns.
Five towns were filled with his relatives.

Early he used to go outside and stay to watch the sun rise.
As the sun was about to rise he spoke to his wife,
"What do you think?
I will go to seek that sun."
His wife said,
"Do you think the sun is *near*, that you can go to it?"

Another day he went out early again.
He saw that sun.
It was just about to rise.
He said to his wife,
"Make moccasins for me. Enough for ten people.
Make leggings for me. Enough for ten people."
So his wife made them.
Enough moccasins and leggings for ten people.

Again it was day. He went.
Far away he went.

He wore out his moccasins.
He wore out his leggings.
He put on another pair of moccasins, another pair of leggings.
Five months he traveled.
He wore out five pairs of moccasins, five pairs of leggings.

Ten months he traveled.
He came near the sun.
He had worn out all his moccasins.
He reached a house, a large house.
He opened the door. There was a girl.
He entered. He stayed.

Then he saw them. There on one side of the house.
Hanging there were arrows.
Hanging there were quivers full of arrows.
Hanging there was elkskin armor.
Hanging there were shields.
Hanging there were stone axes.
Hanging there were bone warclubs.
Hanging there were head ornaments.
All types of men's weapons were on that side of the house.

There on the other side of that house,
Hanging there were mountain-goat blankets.
Hanging there were painted elkskin blankets.
Hanging there were buffalo skins.
Hanging there were dressed buckskins.
Hanging there were long dentalia strands.
Hanging there were shell beads.
Hanging there were short dentalia.
Then, hanging near the door, he saw something large.
He did not know it.

Then he asked that girl,
"Whose things are those, the quivers?"

"My grandmother's things.

　　When I am grown she will give them away."
"Whose things, those wooden armors?"
"My grandmother's things.

　　When I am grown she will give them away."
"Whose things, those shields and those war clubs?"
"My grandmother's things.

　　When I am grown she will give them away."
"Whose things, those stone axes?"
"My grandmother's things.

　　When I am grown she will give them away."
"Whose things, those mountain-goat blankets?"
"My grandmother's things.

　　When I am grown she will give them away."
"Whose things, those buckskins?"
"My grandmother's things.

　　When I am grown she will give them away."
"Whose things, those deerskin blankets?"
"My grandmother's things.

　　When I am grown she will give them away."
"Whose things, those shell beads?"
"My grandmother's things.

　　When I am grown she will give them away."
"Whose things, those long dentalia?"
"My grandmother's things.

　　When I am grown she will give them away."
"Whose things, those short dentalia?"
"My grandmother's things.

　　When I am grown she will give them away."

All those things he asked about.
He thought:
"These things are fine. But that *shining* thing.

　　That is what I want.

　　I will *take* it."

In the evening she came home again, that old woman.
Then she hung it up again, that *thing* that he liked,
that *shining* thing.

He stayed there.
A long time he stayed there.
He stayed with that girl.

Early the old woman left.
In the evenings she came home.
She brought them things.
She brought arrows.
Sometimes mountain-goat blankets.
Sometimes elkskin armors.
All days were like this.
A long time he stayed.
Then homesickness came to him.
For two days he did not rise.
The old woman said to her granddaughter,
"You scolded him and he is angry?"
"No, I did not scold him. It is homesickness."

Then the old woman said to her son-in-law,
"What will you take with you when you go home?
        Those buffalo skins?"
He said to her, "No."
"Those mountain-goat blankets?"
He said to her, "No."
"Those elkskin shirts?"
He said to her, "No."
All that was on one side of the house she showed him.
Then all of the other things she showed him.
She tried to offer him all these things.
He liked that great *thing* that was hanging there.
When it turned round, that *something* hanging up,
he had to close his eyes.

It was shining so, that something.
That, that he wanted.

He said to his wife,
"She shall give me only one thing,
    that blanket,
    her blanket,
    the old woman."
His wife said,
"Never will she give it to you.
    People tried to buy it,
    but she will never give it away."
Then again he became angry.
After several nights the old woman asked him again.
"Will you take this with you?"
She tried to show him all those things.
She showed him those men's things.
She tried to show them all to him.
She reached that *thing* hanging up.
She became silent when she reached that *thing* hanging up.
Then her heart became tired.
She said to him,
"Will you carry it?
    Take care if you carry it!
    You have made up your mind.
    I tried to love you,
    I do love you."
She hung *this* on him.
She put *it* all around him.
Then she gave him a stone axe.
She said to him,
"Go home now."

He went then, he went home.
He saw no country.

He came near to his uncle's town.
Then *it* shook, that which he was wearing.
Then *it* spoke, that which he was wearing.
"We shall strike it, your town.

  We shall strike it, your town!"
That which he was wearing spoke.
His reason left him.
He attacked his town, his uncle's.

  Break! Break! Break!
He did it.
All the people he killed.
He recovered.
All those houses were broken.
His hands were full of blood.
He thought: "Oh, what a fool I was!

  This thing I wanted is BAD!"
He tried to take *it* off.
It stuck to his flesh.

Then again he traveled.
A little while he traveled and he lost his senses again.
He came near to another uncle's town.
Again *it* spoke:
"We shall strike it, your town.

  We shall strike it, your town."
He tried to keep quiet.
It would never stay quiet.
He tried to throw *it* away.
Always his fingers bent to grasp *it*.
Then again, he lost his reason.
Then again, he did this to his uncle's town.

  Break! Break! Break!
All was broken. He did it.
He recovered.
There was nothing left of his uncle's town.

All that were there were dead, the people.
Then he cried.
He tried to strip *it* off on a branch in the tree.
He squeezed himself through.
It did not come off.
It stuck to his flesh.
He struck with a stone at that *thing* he had on.
It did not break at all.

Again he went.
He arrived at another uncle's town.
Again it shook, that *thing* he was wearing.
"We shall strike it, your town.
  We shall strike it, your town."
He lost his reason.
He did it.
His uncle's town.
  Break! Break! Break!
He finished all.
He recovered.
He cried all the time.
He had brought unhappiness to his own relatives.

He tried diving in the water.
It stuck to his flesh.
He tried rolling about in a thicket.
He tried striking *it* with a stone.
He gave up.

Then he cried all the time.
Again he went.
He arrived at another uncle's town.
Again *it* shook.
"We shall strike it, your town.
  We shall strike it, your town."
He lost his senses.

He did it.

    Break! Break! Break! Break! Break!

The town and the people.

He recovered.

Nothing was left of the town and the people.

Only the blood on his arms and hands.

"*Qa! Qa! Qa! Qa!*" he cried.

He tried striking that *thing* he was wearing with stones.

He tried to throw it away.

Always his hands bent to grasp it.

Again he traveled.

Then he came next to his own town.

He came near to his own town.

He tried to stop.

His feet pulled him.

He lost his reason.

He did it.

    Break! Break! Break! Break!

He finished it all.

His town and his relatives, he finished them.

He recovered.

His town was destroyed.

The ground was covered with dead bodies.

He wailed, "*Qa! Qa! Qa! Qa!*"

He tried to bathe.

He tried to get off that *thing* he was wearing.

He struck it with stones.

He thought, "Perhaps it will break."

He gave up.

Then again he cried and wept.

He looked back.

She was standing there, the old woman.

"You." She said to him,

"You.
   I tried to like you.
   I tried to be kind to your relatives.
   Why do you weep?
   You made up your mind.
   You carried it away, that blanket of mine."

Then she took it.
She took it off, that *thing* he was wearing.
She left him. She went home.

He stayed there.
He went a little ways.
He built a small house.

          —A KATHLAMET TALE FROM
            THE PACIFIC NORTHWEST

⁊

Paz con uma espada na mao é guerra.

Peace with a cudgel in hand is war.

          —A PORTUGUESE PROVERB

THE FOLLY OF FIGHTING

THREE FABLES

The Ass's Shadow ◌

A traveler hired a donkey and a driver to take him to the next town.

When they stopped to rest the sun was beating down, and the traveler sat in the donkey's shadow, where there was room for only one person.

"Get up, I want to sit there," said the donkey's owner. "You hired the donkey, not his shadow."

"Nonsense," replied the traveler. "When I hired the donkey that included its shadow."

While the two men were arguing, the donkey ran off.

In quarreling about the shadow we often lose the substance.

—AN AESOP FABLE

The Snipe and
the Mussel 🦪

A mussel was opening its shell to bask in the sun when a snipe
pecked at it. The mussel clamped down on the bird's beak
and held it fast.

"If it doesn't rain today or tomorrow," said the snipe, "there will
be a dead mussel lying here."

"If you can't pry loose today or tomorrow," retorted the mussel,
"there will be a dead snipe here, too."

As neither of them would give way, a passing fisherman caught
them both.

—A TALE FROM CHINA

Fighting Leads to Losses ᐓ

A jackal who was newly married lived near a river bank. One day, his bride asked him for a meal of fish. He promised to bring some, even though he did not know how to swim. He crept up quietly to the river and watched two otters who were struggling with a huge fish they had caught. After killing the fish, the two began to fight about how to divide it.

"I saw it first, so I should have the largest portion!" said one.

"But I saved you when you almost drowned while catching the fish," argued the other.

They continued to fight until the jackal walked up to them and offered to settle the argument. The otters agreed to abide by his decision. He cut the fish in three pieces. To one otter he gave the head, and to the other, the tail. "The middle," he said, "goes to the judge."

He walked away happily, saying, "Fighting always leads to losses."

—A TALE FROM INDIA

ONE WAR

How the Short-ears Conquered the Long-ears &

The Long-ear people were strong; they ruled. They lived out there on Poike, the headland, where the ground is not covered with heavy stones. They stretched their ears with ornaments, those people, they made them hang.

The Short-ears lived on poor land that has many stones. The Long-ears wished to build more ahus near the shore, more ahus for the gods. They said to the Short-ears, "Come and carry stones with us to the place for the ahus; this will make your ground clean." The Short-ears would not do it. They were afraid that the Long-ears would take their land when it was made better.

"We do not want to carry the heavy stones. Leave them on the ground for our food plants, to make them suffer—for the kumara, the banana trees, the sugar canes, to make them suffer and grow."

The Short-ears would not work for the Long-ears; they did not carry them, they left the stones. The Long-ears carried all the stones to build their ahus, angry with the Short-ears.

They built their ahus. They also thought evil against the Short-ears. They dug that long pit which stretches from Potu te rangi to Mahatua; the long pit like an oven. They dug it, they brought firewood, they strewed the whole pit with firewood. The Short-ears did not know for whom the Long-ears were making that oven.

There was a woman of the Short-ears who had a husband of the Long-ear people. She lived at Potu te rangi; that was where she had her house, at that end of the Long-ears' pit. One day her husband in anger said to her, "This pit that is being dug is for all you Short-ears!" He went away angry, left that woman.

Then that woman knew, knew for whom the pit was made. She waited. At night she went to her people, went to the Short-ears and told them:

"Watch my house. Watch it for the sign that I shall give. On the day after tomorrow the Long-ears are to light the oven for your corpses. Form yourselves into a line, make everybody join it, come there, make a circle round the Long-ears, round their land of Poike. Start killing them. Throw them into the pit, change that oven to your own and cook the Long-ears for yourselves."

Before the dawn that woman went back to her house at Potu te rangi. She said to her people, "Be quick and do." Then she went to her house and stayed there, plaiting a basket in the doorway. She was plaiting a basket with her eyes on the Long-ear men. They were filling their oven with firewood.

When it was sunset the Short-ears gathered. It was already dark; they gathered, they came; the first men hid in the house of the woman who was plaiting the basket. The rest concealed them-selves behind; they formed a line, they waited. The woman who was plaiting told them where the Long-ears were. They were in their houses. Therefore the Short-ears went around Kikiriroa and Mount Teatea. They drew up all in order, they marched in the night, they came down to the point of Mahatua. They remained there, they slept, they hid themselves. And at the first light all those Short-ears rose up, they rushed out with their spears and surprised the Long-ear people, they were all still resting in their houses. They rushed and chased, those Short-ear men, they chased the Long-ears out.

They made them all run to the ditch which they had dug themselves. They lit the fires.

When the Short-ears rushed upon them the Long-ears dashed out of their houses: they all ran away, they ran towards the ovens. No other way could the Long-ears run, the Short-ears were behind and all around them. All the wives, all the children of the Long-ears ran, they rushed toward the pit. The men, the women and the children arrived at the pit, stopped there. They were afraid of the flames. The war-party of the Short-ears came up behind them with their spears. Which way could the Long-ears escape from the heat of the fire? There was no way. The war party of the Short-ears came on, they yelled at the Long-ear people.

Then all the Long-ears began jumping into their earth-oven, jumping into the flames. In the flames they jumped, they went on jumping. Their hair was burning; the Long-ears went on jumping. The men, women and children—all were burned.

Two of the Long-ear people stepped over the bodies; these two men jumped and fled across the land. The Short-ears went round the pit and chased them. All the way to Anakena they chased. They arrived at Anakena, those two Long-ears, they ran into Anavai—the cave that has fresh water. They hid themselves in the darkness there.

The Short-ears brought a long stick and they poked it at those Long-ears hidden in the cave, poked and poked. The Long-ears became mad, they showed their faces and jabbered: "Ororoin, Ororoin." It was finished. One of those two died. The other lived, came out; he jabbered. Said one of the Short-ears to the chiefs:

"Important men, let us spare this man who is now alone. Why kill this person? Leave him."

The war party returned to Potu te rangi. They looked at their oven to see whether any of the Long-ears were still living. None remained. All of those people were dead. The Short-ears took as much as they wanted; then they covered them with earth. They returned to their homes.

He remained, that one man of the Long-ear people. He joined

the other people and lived at Turtle Bay. He took a wife and made children. He was the jabbering man of whom they said, "Ka haka-reere mahaki etahi"—"Let us spare this one man only."

I know an old man called Arone arapu; a man of the blood of the Long-ears. The war was in the time of Hotu matua's children.

There are two men alive who are of that blood; one lives at Hangaroa and one is where the lepers are kept: children of the blood of the Long-ears.

—AN HISTORICAL LEGEND FROM POLYNESIA

Ubi solitudinem faciunt,
pacem appellant.

They make a desert and call it peace.

—TACITUS

AN END TO
WAR

The War Between
the Sandpipers
and the Whales 🐚

Every morning little Sandpiper went down to the beach
for her breakfast.
She would run into the water on her tall little legs and
Slup . . . slup . . .
she would peck up a little minnow.
Then she would run back up on the beach and wait.
Into the water she would run again and
Slup . . . slup . . .
gobble up another tidbit.

Whale, who lived in the deep bay, saw Sandpiper running
in and out of the water.
Whale stuck his huge head out of the water
and called to Sandpiper.
    "You! Little bird!
    Stay out of my water!
    The sea belongs to the WHALES!"

Sandpiper just ignored him.
   "The sea belongs to the SANDPIPERS too.
      And there are lots more sandpipers than there are whales.
      So leave me alone!"

Whale was fuming and spewing.
Sandpiper angered him.
   "More SANDPIPERS?
      There are MANY more WHALES in the ocean
      than SANDPIPERS on the LAND!"

"Not SO!" said little Sandpiper.
      There are more SANDPIPERS!"
Whale was furious.
   "I will call my BROTHERS.
      You will see!"

Whale came to the top of the water and spouted
      Buuturu . . . buuturu. . . .
Whale dove deep, deep into the bay.
Whale turned to the east and sounded.
   "Whales of the east.
      Whales of the east.
      Come . . . come to this island!"
Whale came to the top of the water.
He spouted *Buuturu . . . buuturu . . .* and dove to the west.
   "Whales of the west.
      Whales of the west.
      Come . . . come to this island!"

Whale came up again.
He spouted *Buuturu . . . buuturu . . .*
He dove to the north.
   "Whales of the north.
      Whales of the north.
      Come . . . come to this island!"

Whale came up one more time.
He spouted *Buuturu . . . buuturu. . . .*
He dove to the south.

    "Whales of the south.
    Whales of the south.
    Come . . . come to this island!"

In the east, in the west . . .
in the north, in the south . . .
his whale brothers heard.
They began to swim toward that island.
And when they had all come
that bay was so crowded with whales
you could have walked across on their backs!
They were packed so tightly into that bay.

Sandpiper was alarmed.
    "You DO have a lot of brothers.
    But wait.
    I will call my sandpiper sisters!"

Little Sandpiper began to jump up and down
and make her sandpiper call:
    Kirriri. . . . kirriri . . . kirriri. . . . kirriri . . .
    "Sandpipers! Sandpipers!
    East! East! East! East!
    Come quick! Come quick! To this island!

    "Sandpipers! Sandpipers!
    West! West! West! West!
    Come quick! Come quick! To this island!

    "Sandpipers! Sandpipers!
    North! North! North! North!
    Come quick! Come quick! To this island!

"Sandpipers! Sandpipers!
   South! South! South! South!
   Come quick! Come quick! To this island!"

And those sandpipers came flying in!
From the east, the west, the north, the south.
And when they had landed,
those birds covered the entire beach!
They covered the trees!
There were SO many birds.

Were there more birds?
Or more whales?
More whales?
Or more birds?
It was impossible to say.

The whales talked among themselves.
   "We must call our whale COUSINS.
      THEN there will be more sea creatures than BIRDS."

So the whales all came to the top of the water and spouted.
      Buuturu. . . . buuturu . . .
They dove deep, deep.
They called to the east.
   "Cousins to the east.
   Cousins to the east.
   Come . . . come to this island!"
They came up and spouted.
      Buuturu . . . buuturu . . .
They dove.
   "Cousins to the west.
   Cousins to the west.
   Come. Come to this island!"

They came up.
They spouted.
    Buuturu . . . buuturu . . .
They dove.
    "Cousins to the north.
    Cousins to the north.
    Come. Come to this island!"
They came up and spouted.
They dove one more time.
    "Cousins to the south.
    Cousins to the south.
    Come. Come to this island!"

From the east, from the west,
from the north, from the south.
All the whale cousins began to swim toward that island.
Dolphins heard. Dolphins came.
Killer whales heard. Killer whales came.
Porpoises heard. Porpoises came.
Even the sharks came.

When all the whale cousins had arrived
there were so many sea creatures that they surrounded
the island on every side.
As far as you could see in every direction
there were sea creatures spouting and diving.

The sandpipers were frightened.
    "There are SO MANY sea creatures.
    Quick! We must call all of our sandpiper cousins!"

The sandpipers began to jump up and down
and make their call:
    Kirriri . . . kirriri . . . kirriri . . . kirriri . . .

"Sandpiper cousins!
 East! East! East!
 Come quick! Come quick! To this island!

"Sandpiper cousins!
 West! West! West!
 Come quick! Come quick! To this island!

"Sandpiper cousins!
 North! North! North!
 Come quick! Come quick! To this island!

"Sandpiper cousins!
 South! South! South!
 Come quick! Come quick! To this island!"

From the east, from the west,
from the north, from the south,
sandpiper cousins began to arrive.
Gulls heard. Gulls came.
Terns heard. Terns came.
Cormorants heard. Cormorants came.
Even the herons came.

When those seabirds had all arrived
they covered the beaches,
they stretched up into the mountains.
There was not an inch of land on that island
which was not covered by birds!

Were there more birds?
Or more sea creatures?
More whale cousins?
Or more sandpiper cousins?
No one could say.

Then the Whale had an idea.
    "If we whales could eat up the land . . .
      then those birds would drown!
      Then there would be more whales than sandpipers!

    "Let's DO IT!"

The whales began to munch on the beach.
    Scrunch . . . scrunch . . . scrunch . . .
The beach was disappearing into their huge jaws.

Then the Sandpiper had an idea.
    "If we birds drank up all of the sea . . .
      the whales would die!
      THEN there would be more sandpipers than whales!

    "Let's DO IT!"

The birds flew down to the ocean.
Each bird dipped its beak into the sea.
They began to drink.
Those birds drank . . . and drank . . .
their cheeks filled with water. . . .
They drank . . . and drank . . .
their tummies filled with water. . . .
It was easier to drink than to munch.
The birds finished FIRST!

The birds looked down.
The whales lay dying without water.
The fish too all lay gasping.
The tiny crabs . . . the starfish . . . all of the sea creatures . . .
lay dying in the hot sun.

Suddenly the birds thought of something.

"Those tiny crabs . . . these sea creatures . . . that is our FOOD.
This is what we EAT.
If they die . . . WE will die too.
This is a BAD IDEA!
Quick! Spit out the water!
Spit back the ocean!"
Ptoooie . . . ptoooie . . . ptoooie . . .
The birds all spat back the sea.

The whales began to move again.
The fish began to swim about.
The little crabs and the starfish stretched out their legs
and began to live.

"This was a BAD idea!" said the whales.
"The ocean is where we live.
The beach is part of the ocean.
We are destroying our own home.
Quick! Spit back the land."
Glurk. . . . glurk . . . glurk . . .
The whales spat back the beach.

"This war was a bad idea," said Whale.
"There is plenty of ocean for us all to share."

"Yes. A bad idea," agreed Sandpiper.
"We almost destroyed our home!"

And so the whales and their whale cousins all swam away.
To the east, to the west, to the north, to the south.
And the sandpipers and their cousins all flew away.
To the east, to the west, to the north, to the south.
And to this day no one knows.
Are there more whales
or more sandpipers?

Are there more sandpipers
    or more whales?

And after all . . .
    it doesn't really matter.
Such a little thing
    to start a war.

             —A TALE FROM THE
             MARSHALL ISLANDS

૏⚫

Aloha mai no, aloha aku;
o ka huhū ka mea e ola 'ole ai.

When love is given, love should be returned;
anger is the thing which gives no life.

             —A HAWAIIAN PROVERB

The Black Hound ৯

Shakra, king of the gods, arose from his golden throne and peered down towards the earth. There were shining seas and pearl-like clouds, snow-capped mountains and continents of many colors. It was beautiful, yet Shakra felt uneasy.

His luminous senses expanded through the heavens. He felt the heat of war. He heard the bawling of calves, the yelping of dogs, the cawing of crows. He heard children crying. He heard voices shouting in anger. He heard the weeping of the hungry, the lonely, the poor. Tears fell from his eyes, showering the earth like meteors.

"Something must be done!" said Shakra. And he changed himself into a forester with a great horn bow. By his side stood a black hound. The hound's fur was tangled. Its eyes glowed with crimson fire. Its teeth were like fangs. Its mouth and lolling tongue were blood red.

Shakra and his hound leaped, plummeting down down down from among the shining stars. At last they alighted on the earth beside a splendid city.

"Who are you, stranger?" called out an astonished soldier from atop the city's walls.

"I am a forester, and this," said Shakra, with a gesture toward the animal at his side, "is my hound."

The black hound opened its jaws. The soldier on the walls grew dizzy with terror. It was as if he was peering down into a great cauldron of fire and blood. Smoke curled from the hound's throat. Its jaws opened wide, wider still. . . .

"Bar the gates!" shouted the soldier. "Bar them now!"

But Shakra and his hound vaulted over the barred gates. The people of the city fled in every direction, like waves flowing along a beach. The hound bounded after them, herding the people like sheep. Men, women, and children screamed in terror.

"Hold!" called Shakra. "Do not move!" The people stood still. "My hound is hungry. My hound shall feed."

The king of the city, quaking with fear, cried, "Quick! Bring food for the hound! Bring it at once!"

Wagons soon rolled into the market loaded with meat, bread, corn, fruit, and grain. The hound gobbled it all down in a single gulp.

"My hound must have more!" cried Shakra.

Again the wagons rolled. Again the hound gobbled the food down with one gulp. Then it howled a cry of anguish, like a howl from the belly of hell.

The people fell to the ground and covered their ears in fright. Shakra, the forester, plucked his great bow's string. Its sound was like crashing thunder on a stormy night.

"He is still hungry!" cried Shakra. "Feed my hound!"

The king wrung his hands and wept. "He has eaten all we have. There is nothing more!"

"Then," said Shakra, "my hound shall feed on grasses and mountains, on birds and beasts. He shall devour the rocks and gnaw the sun and moon. My hound shall feed on you!"

"No!" cried the people. "Have mercy! We beg you to spare us! Spare our world!"

"Cease war," said Shakra. "Feed the poor. Care for the sick, the homeless, the orphaned, the old. Teach your children kindness and courage. Respect the earth and all its creatures. Only then shall I leash my hound."

Then Shakra grew huge, and he blazed with light. He and his black hound leaped up, curling like smoke as together they rose through the air, higher and higher.

Down below, in the streets of the city, men and women looked up into the skies with dismay. They reached out their hands to one another and vowed to change their lives, vowed to do as the mighty forester had ordered.

From up above, Shakra looked down from his golden throne and smiled. He wiped his brow with a radiant arm. The countless stars blazed with light and the darkness between them slumbered like a dog by the fire.

—A TALE FROM INDIA, RETOLD BY RAFE MARTIN

E moni i ke koko o ka inaina,
`umi ka hanu o ka ho'omanawanui.

Swallow the blood of wrath
and hold the breath of patience.

—A HAWAIIAN PROVERB

2 🐦

PEACE

PATHWAYS TO PEACE

Two Goats on the Bridge ❧

Between two mountains lay a narrow bridge.
On each mountain lived a goat.
Some days the goat from the western mountain would
cross the bridge to graze on the eastern mountain.
Some days the goat from the eastern mountain would
cross the bridge to graze on the western mountain.
But one day both goats began to cross the bridge
at the same time.

The two goats met in the middle of the bridge.
"We have a problem here," said the Western Goat.
"So it seems," said the Eastern Goat.
"I do not want to back up," said the Western Goat.
"Neither do *I*," said the Eastern Goat. "This bridge is narrow,
but perhaps . . ."
"Perhaps if we both are very careful . . . ," added the Western Goat.
" . . . We could pass without FALLING!" concluded the Eastern Goat.

"We can TRY," agreed the two goats.

And cautiously they squeezed past, each being careful not
to overbalance the other.

Thus the goats passed peacefully and went on their way.
Each could be heard to mutter,
"What a cooperative fellow *he* is!"
—A TALE FROM EASTERN EUROPE

Jos ei Pääse lapi,
kävelle ympäri.

If you can't get through,
walk around.
—A FINNISH PROVERB

How Friendship Began Among Birds ⧫

At first friendship was unknown among birds, for there was an intense rivalry among them all. If a bird saw another bird, he at once said, "I am a better bird than you." Then they would start to fight.

One day the Pheasant met the Crow and, being in no mood to quarrel, he said, "Crow, you are a better bird than me."

The Crow was not only surprised but very pleased at these words of the Pheasant, and out of politeness, he replied, "No, no, Pheasant, you are a better bird than I." The two birds sat down and had a chat.

Then the Pheasant said to the Crow, "Crow, I like you. Let us stay together."

"All right, Pheasant," replied the Crow. So the two lived together in a big tree. With the passing of time, their regard for each other grew, but in their case familiarity did not breed contempt, and they continued to show courtesy and respect to each other.

Other birds watched the association of the Pheasant and the Crow with interest, and they were surprised that the two birds should stay together for such a long time without fighting or quarreling. At last some of the birds decided to test their friendship. So they went to the Pheasant while the Crow was away, and said, "Pheasant, why do you live with that good-for-nothing Crow?"

"You must not say that," replied the Pheasant, "the Crow is a better bird than I, and he honors me by living with me in this tree."

The next day they went to the Crow while the Pheasant was away and said, "Crow, why do you live with that good-for-nothing Pheasant?"

"You must not say that," replied the Crow. "The Pheasant is a better bird than I, and he honors me by living with me in this tree."

The birds were deeply impressed with the attitude of the Pheasant and the Crow towards each other, and they said to themselves, "Why couldn't we be like the Pheasant and the Crow, instead of fighting and quarreling?" And from that day onwards, friendship and respect for one another developed among the birds.

—A TALE FROM BURMA

Gleich und gleich fängt keinen Krieg an.

Equality breeds no war.

—A GERMAN PROVERB

The Lion's Whisker 🐾

Bizunesh, a woman of the African highlands, married Gudina, a man of the lowlands. When Bizunesh went to the house of Gudina, she found that he had a son named Segab. Segab was a very sad boy because his mother had died of the fever.

Bizunesh loved Segab very much and tried to be a true mother. She mended all of Segab's robes. She patched Segab's shoes. She always asked him which food he liked best. And she always tried to save the choicest pieces of meat from the stew for Segab. But he did not thank her. He did not even speak to her.

Bizunesh and her new son, Segab, were often alone together in the house of Gudina. Gudina was a merchant and traveled with mule caravans to distant cities in the mountains and on the plains. When Bizunesh was alone with Segab, she would speak to him very kindly. "I have always wanted a small son. Now God has given me one. I love you very much." She often tried to kiss him.

Segab would run from her and shout in a cross voice, "I do not love you. You are not my real mother. My mother is dead. I do not love you. I hate you."

Bizunesh would try to cook the food that Segab loved best. But Segab would not eat the food. She mended his robes, and he would run through the thorn bushes and tear the clothes. He waded in the river and ruined his new shoes. Every time she tried to kiss Segab, he would run away from her. Often she cried alone in her room, and she longed for the day when her son would love her as she loved him.

One day Segab ran away from the house, and stayed in the forest until his father came and found him. When Segab came home, he would not let his stepmother kiss him. Bizunesh cried all that night.

In the morning, Bizunesh went to the cave of a very famous wise man. Bizunesh told the wise man about her new son who did not love her. She said, "You must make me a magic love powder. Then Segab will love me, as he loved his own mother."

The wise man said, "To make such a powder I must have the chin whiskers of an old and ferocious lion who walks in the black-rock desert beyond the river. Bring the whiskers to me."

"How can I do that?" Bizunesh asked. "The lion will kill me."

"I cannot answer that," said the wise man. "I know about love powders. But I know little about lions. You must find a way."

Now Bizunesh loved Segab very much. She decided that she would try to get the chin whiskers, danger or not.

Bizunesh crossed the river to the black-rock desert and looked at the lion from afar. The lion was a fierce one. When he roared, Bizunesh was afraid, and she ran away home.

The next day Bizunesh came from her house carrying food. She placed the food on a rock a mile away from the lion and ran.

On the following day, Bizunesh brought food and left it only a half-mile from the lion. On the next day, Bizunesh left the food a quarter of a mile from the lion and watched him from a distance while he ate.

Finally, Bizunesh left the food only a hundred yards from the fierce lion. The lion saw her and growled in a friendly way. Bizunesh stayed while the lion ate the food. The next day she left the food fifty yards from the lion. Then one day Bizunesh went right up to the lion and fed him. She watched the lion's great jaw fly open! Crash shut! She heard the sound of his teeth tearing through the meat. She was very much frightened. But she loved Segab very much. She shut her eyes and reached out and snatched the whiskers from the lion's chin. The lion hardly noticed the small pain of losing three of his chin whiskers. Bizunesh ran away to the wise man's cave.

She was almost out of breath when she reached the cave. "I have the lion's whiskers," she cried. "Now make me the love powder, and Segab will surely love me."

"I will not make you any love powder," the wise man said. "You learned how to approach the lion—slowly. Do the same with Segab, and he will surely learn to love you."

—A SOMALI TALE FROM ETHIOPIA

Nasake ni hamukau yaiba nashi.

There is no blade that can offer resistance to kindness.

—A JAPANESE PROVERB

CONTROL OF TEMPER

Temper

AZen student came to Bankei and complained: "Master, I have an ungovernable temper. How can I cure it?"

"You have something very strange," replied Bankei. "Let me see what you have."

"Just now I cannot show it to you," replied the other.

"When can you show it to me?" asked Bankei.

"It arises unexpectedly," replied the student.

"Then," concluded Bankei, "it must not be your own true nature. If it were, you could show it to me at any time. When you were born you did not have it, and your parents did not give it to you. Think that over."

—A ZEN TALE

Hito-goto iwan yori waga hachi harae.

Instead of talking about other people's affairs,
let me drive off my own wasps.

—A JAPANESE PROVERB

The Advice of Hatim al-Asamm

H atim al-Asamm was from Balk, a city located in present-day
Afghanistan. When he once visited Baghdad he made quite
an impression on the people there. They gathered around
him and said, "You are a non-Arab of halting speech, yet you silence
everyone." He answered, "Three things enable me to overcome my
opponent. I am happy when he is right, and I am sad when he is
wrong, and I try not to behave foolishly towards him."

Hearing this, Ibn Hanbal asked Hatim what things would save
humanity from the world. He replied, "There are four things. Accept
the ignorance of others and spare them yours; spare for them from
your substance, and do not expect any of theirs."

—A SUFI ANECDOTE

Ju yoku go wo seisu.

Gentleness skillfully subdues wrath.

—A JAPANESE PROVERB

Music to Soothe the Savage Breast

A musician named Mochimitsu was on his way home from a trip to Tosa province when, at a harbor in Aki, he was attacked by pirates. Having no skill at arms, he was quite unable to defend himself and was sure he was going to be killed.

He had taken refuge on top of his ship's cabin. At the last moment he took out his *hichiriki* and shouted, "You pirates, listen to me! I'm defenseless, as you can see. Help yourselves to anything you want! But I'd just like you to hear this piece on the *hichiriki*. I've been working on it for years. It'll be something for you to remember today by!"

"All right, men!" shouted the pirates' leader. "Hold it! We're going to listen to some music!"

When the pirates had quieted down, the weeping Mochimitsu began to play. This was the last time he would ever make music, and he poured his whole soul into the piece. The beautiful sound of his instrument floated far out over the waves and filled the bay where the ship was moored. It was just like a scene in an old tale.

The pirates listened in perfect silence. When the music was over, their leader loudly declared, "I came because I wanted your ship, but your playing has brought tears to my eyes. I couldn't possibly harm you now!"

The pirates rowed away.

—AN HISTORICAL LEGEND FROM JAPAN

Todo el mundo sonrie en el mismo idioma.
All the world smiles in the same language.
—A MEXICAN PROVERB

CONSIDERATION

Slops 🙶

There once was an old man and an old woman who lived in a house with a garden wall all around it.
Every evening the old woman would cook the dinner.
First she would peel the potatoes . . .
and toss the peelings in the slop bucket.
Then she would peel the carrots . . .
and toss the peelings in the slop bucket.
Then she would peel the onions . . .
and toss the peelings in the slop bucket.
And later, when dinner was over
she would wash the dishes up
and pour the dirty dishwater into the slop bucket.

Then the old man would pick up that heavy bucket
and carry it acro-o-oss the floor . . .
out the front door . . .
one, two, three, four, five, six, seven, eight, nine, ten
steps to the front garden wall
and throw the slops over the wall
SLOSH!

One evening when the old man carried the slop bucket
across the yard . . .
one, two, three, four, five, six, seven, eight, nine, ten
steps . . .
SLOSH!
he heard a shrill little voice
"I *wish* you would stop doing that!
How I *wish* you would stop doing that!"

He looked all around, but didn't see a thing.

The old man went back in the house puzzled
and told his wife what he had heard.
"Could it have been one of the wee folk?" she wondered.
"I don't know, but whoever it was, they didn't seem
to want me to pour out the slops."

The next night the old woman peeled her potatoes as usual . . .
and tossed the peelings in the slop bucket.
She peeled her carrots . . .
and tossed the peelings in the slop bucket.
She peeled her onions . . .
and tossed the peelings in the slop bucket.
She washed her dishes . . .
and poured the dirty dishwater into the slop bucket.
Then the old man picked up the heavy bucket . . .
carried it acro-o-oss the floor . . .
out the door . . .
one, two, three, four, five, six, seven, eight, nine, ten
steps . . .
and threw it over the front garden wall
SLOSH!

"OOOOHHHH I *wish* you would stop doing that!
I *wish* you would stop doing that!"

This time the old man looked all around.
There at his feet stood a tiny little man with a red feather
in his hat.
"*Must* you pour slops down my chimney every single day?!"
"What ever are you talking about?" said the old man.
"I pour my slops over the garden wall into that empty field.
They don't go down anyone's chimney."
"Look again," said the little man.
"Don't you see my house?"
The old man looked over the garden wall.

He looked all about.
All he saw were weeds and stones.
The old man went back into his house very confused.
He told his wife about the little man.
"What can he be talking about?
He seems to want me to throw the slops somewhere else.
But the slop bucket is so heavy I can barely take it to the
    front garden wall.
    I couldn't carry it farther than that."

So the next evening the old woman made the supper as usual.
She peeled the potatoes
    and tossed the peelings in the slop bucket.
She peeled the carrots
    and tossed the peelings in the slop bucket.
She peeled the onions
    and tossed the peelings in the slop bucket.
She washed the dishes
    and poured the dirty dishwater into the slop bucket.

Then the old man hoisted the heavy bucket . . .
    carried it acro-o-oss the floor . . .
    out the door . . .
    one, two, three, four, five, six, seven, eight, nine, ten
    steps . . .
and threw the slops over the front garden wall
    SLOSH!

"OOOOOHHHHH NOOOOO, you're doing it AGAIN!
I *wish* you'd stop doing that!"
There was the little man.
"You are pouring your slops right down my chimney!"
"Well, I hear what you are saying," said the old man,
"But I don't see a house on the other side of this fence.
I see nothing but weeds and stones."

"If you could only see with *my* eyes, " said the little man.
"Would you be willing to look with my eyes, if you could?"
"Oh yes, I'd be willing to do that," said the old man.
"Then put your foot on top of my foot."
The old man looked down at the little man's feet.
Suddenly he saw that they were very large feet indeed.
Gently he put his own big foot right on top of the
    little man's foot.
"Now look over the wall."

The old man peered over the wall.
There was a tiny village!
Right on the other side of his garden wall.
And at the spot where he always poured out his slops . . .
    there was a wee cottage.
But oh, what a mess it was!

There were potato peelings all over the roof.
Carrot peelings hung from the windows.
The yard was piled with onion skins.
And dirty dishwater was running down the chimney and
    out the front door.

"I've been pouring my slops down your *chimney*!" said the old man.
"That's what I've been trying to *tell* you.
I *wish* you would stop doing that!"

The old man went back into his house and told his wife
    just what he had seen.
"And the little man's wife has to mop up the dirty dishwater and
  sweep out the potato peelings *every* single day,"
    explained the old man.
"That poor woman! We must *stop* pouring our slops down her
    chimney!" said the old woman.
"But where shall we pour them?" said the old man.

"I cannot carry the slop bucket around the house to the
        back garden wall. It is much too heavy."

They sat and thought.
There must be a way to solve this.
They thought and thought.

At last the old woman had an idea.
"If we had a door in the *back* of the house," she said,
"You could carry the slop bucket ten steps out the *back* door
    and throw the slops over the *back* garden wall.
    Then the little man's village by the front garden wall would
        be saved from our slops."
"We could hire the village carpenter to make us a new back door,"
    said the old man. "But it would cost a bit."
"I have some money saved," said the old woman.
"And I will be glad to spend it for a door, if it will save
        that poor little man's wife the trouble of mopping up
        our slops every day!"

So the carpenter was called.
He built a fine door at the *back* of the house.
And he boarded up the front door.
"So no one can ever again pour slops on the little man's
        village," said the old man.

That night the old woman prepared supper as usual.
She peeled her potatoes
    and tossed the peelings in the slop bucket.
She peeled her carrots
    and tossed the peelings in the slop bucket.
She peeled her onions
    and tossed the peelings in the slop bucket.
She washed the dishes
    and poured the dirty dishwater into the slop bucket.

Then the old man hoisted the heavy slop bucket . . .

    carried it acro-o-oss the floor . . .

    out the door . . .

    one, two, three, four, five, six, seven, eight, nine, ten

    steps . . .

and threw it over the BACK garden wall

    SLOSH!

And though they had spent their savings on the new back door,
the old man and the old woman never wanted for anything again.
Because every night when he pushed open the new back door

    clink . . . clink . . . clink . . . clink . . . clink . . .

A tiny silver coin would roll out from under the door.
It was left there by the little man . . .

    a gift . . .

from one good neighbor to another.

                             —A TALE FROM WALES

Begossen Gras wächst am besten.

Friendship is a plant which must often be watered.

                              —A GERMAN PROVERB

INTERVENTION

Nansen Cuts
the Cat in Two

Nansen saw the monks of the eastern and western halls fighting over a cat. He seized the cat and told the monks, "If any of you say a good word, you can save the cat."

No one answered. So Nansen boldly cut the cat in two pieces.

That evening Joshu returned and Nansen told him about this. Joshu removed his sandals and, placing them on his head, walked out.

Nansen said, "If you had been there, you could have saved the cat."

—A ZEN TALE

Del dicho al heco hay mucho trecho.

From the word to the deed is a long way.

—A MEXICAN PROVERB

REPAYING EVIL WITH KINDNESS

A Lesson for Kings 🌿

The King of Benares and the King of Kosala once met on the road. Each sat erect in his chariot, taking the middle of the road. Each refused to make way for the other.

The charioteer of the King of Benares thought to solve this dilemma by letting the older of the two pass first. But on inquiry he found both to be of the same age.

Next he inquired about the extent of their kingdoms. Both ruled kingdoms of three hundred leagues. In wealth and family they were also matched.

At last he thought, "I will make way for the most righteous." And he asked, "What kind of righteousness has this king of yours?"

The charioteer of the King of Kosala proclaimed his king's virtues thus:

"The strong he overthrows by strength.
The mild by mildness.
The good he conquers by goodness,
and the wicked by wickedness too.
Such is the nature of this king!
Move out of the way, O charioteer!"

But the charioteer of the King of Benares was not impressed.

"If these are his *virtues*, what are his *faults*?" And he began to recite the virtues of the King of Benares.

"Anger he conquers by calmness,
 and by goodness the wicked.
 The stingy he conquers by gifts,
 and by truth the speaker of lies.
 Such is the nature of *this* king!
 Move out of the way, O charioteer!"

And when the King of Kosala heard this, he and his charioteer came down from their chariot and made way for the King of Benares.

—A JATAKA TALE FROM INDIA

Lemah liat kayu akar,
di-lentok boleh,
di-patah ta'dapat.

[A diplomat should be]
yielding and supple as a liana
that can be bent but not broken.

—A MALAY PROVERB

Heaven and Hell

A man once asked to visit heaven and hell. When he reached hell he was amazed to find people seated around a huge banquet table. The finest foods were piled high on the table. What a feast! Perhaps hell was not so bad after all!

But when he looked closely at the diners he saw that they were all starving despite the food before them. You see, each diner had been given chopsticks which were *three feet long*! There was no way they could carry the food to their mouths with these long chopsticks. No one could eat a bite. What a hell indeed, to sit so close to a banquet and yet be unable to taste a morsel.

The man was then taken to heaven to observe life there. To his surprise he saw people seated around a banquet table in exactly the same situation. Each person had been given three-foot-long chopsticks in heaven too! But here everyone was happily consuming the delicious food. The residents of heaven . . . were using their yardlong chopsticks to feed *each other*.

—A TALE FROM CHINA

Ilo on rauhan tytär.

Joy is the daughter of peace.
　　　—A FINNISH PROVERB

A Blind Man Catches a Bird ❧

A young man married a woman whose brother was blind. The young man was eager to get to know his new brother-in-law and so he asked him if he would like to go hunting with him.

"I cannot see," the blind man said. "But you can help me see when we are out hunting together. We can go."

The young man led the blind man off into the bush. At first they followed a path that he knew and it was easy for the blind man to tag on behind the other. After a while, though, they went off into thicker bush, where the trees grew closely together and there were many places for animals to hide. The blind man now held on to the arm of his sighted brother-in-law and told him many things about the sounds that they had heard around them. Because he had no sight, he had a great ability to interpret the noises made by animals in the bush.

"There are warthogs around," he would say. "I can hear their noises over there."

Or, "That bird is preparing to fly. Listen to the sound of its wings unfolding."

To the brother-in-law, these sounds were meaningless, and he was most impressed at the blind man's ability to understand the bush although it must have been for him one great darkness.

They walked on for several hours, until they reached a place where they could set their traps. The blind man followed the other's advice, and put his trap in a place where birds might come for water. The other man put his trap a short distance away, taking care to disguise it so that no bird would know that it was there. He did not bother to disguise the blind man's trap, as it was hot and he was eager to get home to his new wife. The blind man thought that he had disguised his trap, but he did not see that he had failed to do so and any bird could tell that there was a trap there.

They returned to their hunting place the next day. The blind man was excited at the prospect of having caught something, and the young man had to tell him to keep quiet, or he would scare all the animals away. Even before they had reached the traps, the blind man was able to tell that they had caught something.

"I can hear birds," he said. "There are birds in the traps."

When he reached his trap, the young man saw that he had caught a small bird. He took it out of the trap and put it in a pouch that he had brought with him. Then the two of them walked towards the blind man's trap.

"There's a bird in it," he said to the blind man. "You have caught a bird too."

As he spoke, he felt himself filling with jealousy. The blind man's bird was marvelously colored, as if it had flown through a rainbow and been stained by the colors. The feathers from a bird such as that would make a fine present for his new wife, but the blind man had a wife too, and she would also want the feathers.

The young man bent down and took the blind man's bird from the trap. Then, quickly substituting his own bird, he passed it to the blind man and put the colored bird in his own pouch.

"Here is your bird," he said to the blind man. "You may put it in your pouch."

The blind man reached out for the bird and took it. He felt it for a moment, his fingers passing over the wings and the breast. Then, without saying anything, he put the bird into his pouch and they began the trip home.

On their way home, the two men stopped to rest under a broad tree. As they sat there, they talked about many things. The young man was impressed with the wisdom of the blind man, who knew a great deal, although he could see nothing at all.

"Why do people fight with one another?" he asked the blind man. It was a question which had always troubled him and he wondered if the blind man could give him an answer.

The blind man said nothing for a few moments, but it was clear to the young man that he was thinking. Then the blind man raised his head, and it seemed to the young man as if the unseeing eyes were staring right into his soul. Quietly he gave his answer.

"Men fight because they do to each other what you have just done to me."

The words shocked the young man and made him ashamed. He tried to think of a reponse, but none came. Rising to his feet, he fetched his pouch, took out the brightly-colored bird and gave it back to the blind man.

The blind man took the bird, felt it over with his fingers, and smiled.

"Do you have any other questions for me?" he asked.

"Yes," said the young man. "How do men become friends after they have fought?"

The blind man smiled again.

"They do what you have just done," he said. "That's how they become friends again."

—A NDEBELE TALE FROM ZIMBABWE

T'a ch'ou, wo pu ch'ou,
yuan chia chi liao hsiu.

Although he hates me,
if I do not hate him
enmity will soon be at an end.

—A CHINESE PROVERB

Old Joe and the Carpenter ⁊

Old Joe lived way out in the countryside, and he had one good neighbor. They'd been friends all their lives long. It seemed that they had grown old together. And now that their spouses were dead and buried and their children raised and living lives of their own in other places, all they had left were their farms . . . and each other.

But for the first time in their long relationship, they'd had an argument. And it was a silly argument. It was over a stray calf that neither one really needed. It seemed as though the calf was found on Joe's neighbor's land and so he claimed it as his own. But Old Joe said, "No, no, now that calf has the same markings as my favorite cow, and I recognize it as being mine."

Well, they were both a bit stubborn, so the upshot of it was they just stopped talking to each other. That happened about a week before, and it seemed that a dark cloud had settled over Old Joe . . . until there came a knock on his door.

He wasn't expecting anybody that morning, and as he opened the door, he saw standing before him a young man who had a box of wooden tools on his shoulder. He had a kind voice and rather dark, deep eyes, and he said, "I'm just a carpenter, and I'm looking for a bit of work. Maybe you'd have some small jobs here and there that I can help with."

Old Joe wasn't the kind of fellow to take someone on just right off, so he brought him on into the kitchen and sat him down and gave him some stew that he had on the back of the stove. There was some homemade bread (it was baked fresh early that morning), some fresh churned butter, and homemade jam. While they were sitting and eating and talking, Joe decided that he liked this young fellow, and he said, "I do have a job for you. Look right there through my kitchen window. See that farm over there across the way? That's my neighbor's place. And you see that crick running right down there between our property lines? That crick, it wasn't there last week. My neighbor did that to spite me, dadburn it. He took his plow up there with a tractor, and he just dug a big old furrow from the upper pond and then he flooded it.

"Well, I want you to do one better. Since he wants us divided that way, you go out there and build me a fence—a big, tall fence—so I won't even have to *see* his place no more. Goldurn him anyhow!"

And the carpenter said, "Well, if you have the lumber and the nails, I got my tools, and I'll be able to do a job that you'll like."

Joe had to go on to town to get some supplies, so he hitched up the wagon and showed the carpenter where everything was in the barn . . . and that carpenter, well he carried everything he needed down to the crick side and he started to work.

And, oh, his work, it went smooth and fast. He did his measuring and his sawing and his nailing . . . and it was about sunset when Old Joe returned and the carpenter had finished his work. And when Old Joe pulled up in that wagon, his eyes opened wide and his mouth fell open . . . because there wasn't a fence there at all.

It was a bridge, going from one side of the crick to the other! It had handrails and all—a fine piece of work—and his neighbor was just starting to cross the other side of that bridge with his hand stuck out, and he was saying, "Joe, you're quite a fellow to build this bridge. I'da never been able to do that. I'm so glad we're going to be friends again!"

And Joe, he put his arms around his neighbor and he said, "Oh, that calf is *yours*. I've known it all the time. I just want to be your friend, too."

About that time, the carpenter started putting his tools in the box and then hoisted it up onto his shoulder, and he started to walk away. And Joe said, "No, now wait, come on back, young fellow. I want you to stay on. I got lots of projects for you."

The carpenter just smiled and said, "I'd like to stay on, Joe, but you see, I can't. I got *more* bridges to build."

So he walked on, and there ends my tale.

—A TALE FROM THE UNITED STATES,
RETOLD BY PLEASANT DeSPAIN

🙋

Dost bin ise azdir,
Düsman bir ise çoktur.

One thousand friends are too little,
One enemy is too many.

—A TURKISH PROVERB

Two Foxes 🥀

In a dark, busy forest in Virginia, where rabbits made eggs for Easter and toads make warts for silly people, lived two foxes. They lived near a spring from which ran a little rivulet that gave water to the animals that lived in the woods.

They were two very beautiful foxes. One was a little older than the other, and they were the best of friends. Their friendship was made of fire and water, the two great riches in the world, and so nothing could break that friendship. Other animals in those woods gossiped about it, but just as barking couldn't harm the moon, all the gossip couldn't break the friendship of these two foxes. They went their way in peace and pleasure as God wanted them to live.

Yet, though the golden sun shines warm in the day, there is the dark night with cold winds. There was no end of animals and insects in the woods and the two friends saw and heard fussing and quarreling all around them.

One day the two foxes were talking pleasantly to each other.

"It is good to be like everybody," said the taller of the two. "Maybe we should try fussing and fighting, then we too will be like everyone else."

"Maybe you are right and we should be like all other folks. I think I would like that."

"Come, let us start," said the taller.

"How do we start?"

"Let me think," said the taller. His long thick tail went down and so did his long snout. For a time he was looking down on the little running water and the glittering stones lying around.

"We could bite each other," said the taller. "I have seen many animals biting each other when they are angry."

"No, it would hurt," said the smaller.

"Yes, it would hurt. I am bigger than you and you are my friend and I don't want to hurt you. Maybe it would be better to get into an argument first and get angry at each other like everybody else."

"That would be better," said the smaller fox. "How do we do that?"

"Well, here are two nice stones lying in the water. I'll show you how we start."

He picked up the two gleaming stones with his paws. Then, raising his voice, he screamed just as he heard the others do.

"These two white stones are my stones. You can't have them, do you hear me?"

"Yes, I heard you," said the other. "If they are your stones, then they are your stones. I don't want to take anything from you. You keep them."

For a time the tall fox was quiet. "We are not getting anywhere with our quarreling," he said, a little downhearted.

"No, we are not, good friend fox."

"Well, let us try again. Let us try another way. Maybe we can do better." They were quiet for a little time, then the older raised his long snout and bushy tail and said in a loud voice, "This wood belongs to me and you had better get out of it quick."

Said the other, "I am sorry, I like you and I like you to be my friend. But if this is your wood and you want it, I will have to go out even if I don't want to. It is a nice wood and I like it. Now I will have to find another."

The tall fox looked at his friend in surprise. He liked his friend and did not want to hurt him.

"I don't want you to go. We are good friends and we like to be together and play with each other."

"I am happy to hear you say that. I didn't want to go. I want to be with you."

The two were silent for a time, then the taller said:

"Friend, we are not good at fussing and fighting and quarreling. I think it is best for us to be as we are. Let us be the way we are, not the way others are."

So these two foxes in the deep wood remained, all their lives, good friends instead of fighting enemies. And I am glad they did.

—A TALE FROM APPALACHIA

Aite no nai kenka wa dekinu.

When there is no one against you,
you cannot quarrel.

—A JAPANESE PROVERB

Lifting the Sky ❧

A long time ago,
the Creator was traveling.
As he traveled, his face was shining SO brightly
nobody could see his face.

As he traveled,
he carried in his hands *many, many* languages.
And to each group he gave a very special language.
Everywhere he walked
he presented that group with a *very special* language.

He arrived at the Puget Sound area—in *my country.*
He stood and he looked around.
"This is such *beautiful, beautiful* land.
I need go *no* further.
I can stop *right here.*
Because this is the most beautiful land in the world."

And in his hands he still carried *many, many* languages.
So now he *tossed* these languages in all directions.
Now the people didn't understand one another.
There were so many different languages.
And the Creator had left the sky too low.
Tall people were bumping their heads against the sky.
And some of them were climbing into the Sky World.
And this was not appropriate.
There was a time to go into the Sky World and not just whenever
you felt like it.

"How in the world can we fix this problem?"
the people worried.

"The Creator has left the sky too low.
And we all *don't* understand one another.
How can we fix this problem when we *don't* have a common
language?"

Now wise people gathered.
And they said to the listening people,
"There is a way.
We can all learn *one* word . . . *one* word . . .
YA-HOW!
It means to proceed—to go ahead.
We could each prepare a *long, long* pole
and we could fix this problem."

"Each one of us is going to fix a *long, long* pole.
There are still trees that can be made into long, long poles.
So each one of you will help.
You know the word . . .
YA-HOW!
Now you are preparing for yourself a long pole.
And everything happens four times.
That is the magic number."

So now all the people have been gathered.
They have *all* learned this one word.
"Now you are going to put your poles to the sky.
All together . . ."

"YA-HOW!"
The sky only went up a little bit.

"Everyone has to put their backs to their poles."

"YA..A..A..HOW!"
The sky only went up a little further.

"Who is not pushing?
 We have to push harder.
 And maybe you all have to use a *BIG* voice."

"YA..A..A..HOW!"
 It went up a little further.

"Four times.
 Maybe someone is still not pushing hard enough.
 This is the last time."

"YA..A..A..A..HOW!"
"OOOHHHH! We DID it!"

 Because everybody worked with one heart,
 with one mind,
 with a common goal
 you pushed the sky up where it still is today.

However
 while people were doing this there were some hunters
 chasing some elk and they weren't paying *any* attention
 to what was going on around them.
 And the elk jumped into the Sky World as the sky was being
 pushed up and the hunters jumped after them.
 And they got stuck up in that Sky World and they are
 the Big Dipper
 up there in the sky.

 There also were some fishermen.
 They were fishing and not paying any attention
 to what was going on around them.
 And as the sky was being lifted
 they got *stuck* up in that Sky World and they became
 the skatefish that is still up there in the Sky World.

So of course we are told
"Always be alert.
Always be alert . . ."

Work together
and work towards a common cause
and you can do a lot with *one* word.

—A SKAGIT TALE FROM THE PACIFIC NORTHWEST
AS TOLD BY SKAGIT ELDER VI (TAQʷŠƎBLU) HILBERT

*Zarreh zarreh jam garadad
vangahi darya shavad.*

Drops that gather one by one
finally become a sea.

           —A PERSIAN PROVERB

PEACEMAKING TECHNIQUES

PEACEMAKING TECHNIQUE #1

Halving the Cookie ❧

Problem: One cookie.
              Two kids.

Solution: One kid divides the cookie in half.
              The other kid gets first choice of halves.

—AMERICAN FOLK ADVICE

The Argument Sticks 🍂

Two Iroquois boys were arguing.
Neither would admit he was wrong.
They were about to come to blows over this.

Their mother gave them three sticks:
"These are special Argument Sticks.
They will solve this argument for you.
Set your sticks up in the woods,
leaning one against the other so they all stand up.
Leave them there for one month.
If they fall over toward the north,
the one who sets up the northern stick
is right in this matter.
If they fall over toward the south,
the one who sets up the southern stick
is right in this matter."

The boys took their sticks into the woods and set them up.
They were satisfied that this would solve their argument.
A month later the boys remembered their Argument Sticks.
They went into the woods to find out
who had won the argument.

The sticks had fallen in a heap and begun to rot.
There was no winner.

And the boys couldn't remember what the argument
had been about in the first place.

—AN IROQUOIS TALE

Looking Your Enemy in the Eye ❧

Here is a peacemaking technique that worked for one Indiana mother.

Her daughter says:

I have two younger sisters. If any of us got in a fight while playing, my mother would sometimes resolve the conflict as follows.

Drawing up two chairs, facing each other about a foot apart, she ordered the two adversaries to sit. "Now you have to look at each other for five minutes," she said. And she stood there to make sure we did, saying, "Jennifer, look at your sister," in that this-is-your-mother voice that no child dares defy. Faces set, we lifted our heads to stare frostily at the other's crossed arms. "Look at her face. Look her in the eye," my mother ordered. We grudgingly complied, struggling to maintain our angry scowls, trying not to smile at the hilarious scowl on the other's face. Of course these efforts resulted in even more hilarious facial contortions, and as we watched each other it became impossible not to smile. Before we knew it we were both laughing out loud at each other and ourselves, and our stern judge was smiling and trying not to crack up laughing herself. "You may go now," she said as solemnly as she could, then retreated to the kitchen to laugh quietly to herself while we scooted back to our play.

We never had to sit there the full five minutes.

Now I'm sure this approach didn't work for every conflict. I remember that at times punishment was meted out instead in cases where physical harm was involved, for example. But I remember squirming on that chair, trying so hard to hold onto my anger and finding it impossible when I really looked at who I was angry with.

—AN AMERICAN FAMILY CUSTOM

PEACEMAKERS

Buddha
Prevents a War ૨

Upon a certain occasion Buddha prevented a war which was on the point of breaking out between the Shakyas and the Kolis. Between the cities of Kapilavastu and Koli ran the river Rohini; across this river a dam had been built which enabled the people of both countries to irrigate their fields. It so happened that there was a great drought, and the husbandmen on each side claimed the sole right to the little water that remained. The rival claimants called each other by the worst possible names; and the matter, coming to the ears of the princes of each country, much exaggerated by rumor, led to the outbreak of war, and matters had gone so far that the armies of the Shakyas and the Kolis were encamped over against each other on opposite banks of the diminished river.

At this crisis Buddha perceived what was going on, and proceeding through the air, at the same time making himself visible, he arrived at the place of battle. The Shakyas threw down their weapons out of respect for him whom they regarded as the jewel of their race, and the Kolis followed their example. Buddha inquired if they were assembled for a water-festival, and being informed that it was for

89

battle, asked the cause. The princes said that they were not quite sure, but would inquire of the generals; they in turn asked their under-officers, and so on downward until it came to the original husbandmen.

When Buddha was informed of the cause he asked the value of the water, and being told that it was very little, he asked what was the value of men, and was told that it was very great.

"Why then," he asked, "do you propose to throw away that which is of great value for the sake of that of little value?" This convincing argument sufficed to end the matter.

—A TALE FROM INDIA

El respeto al derecho ajeno
es la paz.

Respect for the rights of another,
that is peace.

—A MEXICAN-AMERICAN PROVERB

The Battle ❧

They were so angry that they decided to have a battle. So terrible was their anger that they would not wait, but decided that the fight must be fought now, immediately, on this very spot. Fox blamed what he considered to be the crime on Badger. Badger in turn was all for placing the blame on Cougar.

Jackrabbit hopped in agitation, calling for Mole and for Mouse, and for Deer and Bear to fetch their sharpest arrows and their heaviest warclubs.

By the time Coyote arrived the sides had already been chosen, the battle lines formed, and the smell of hate and future bloodshed permeated the very air.

He, Coyote, listened to all the threats and promises of broken bodies to be. He walked out and stood between the enemies, declaring very solemnly, and in a very soft voice:

"No, I cannot allow this great fight to happen just yet. There has been no battle-preparation dance. There has been no pipe of cleansing. No, the Creator does not wish this battle to take place just yet."

And some say it was Bear, but strangely, no one actually remembers just who it was. Bear denied the accusation, but someone ran from one of the lines and struck Coyote dead!

And Coyote fell and indeed lay there, very dead. And the cry for immediate battle resumed, and the menacing cries for blood again filled the air, when, from the opposite end of the battle lines, Coyote again stepped out, dancing and brandishing a huge club. He ran to his dead self and struck a tremendous blow upon the body, then turned to face the creatures, shouting:

"Who killed this person? Who struck him down before I did? Was that person purified? Did he sweat himself and think of the children? Did he dance to assure that the life cycle continue?"

"Enough talking!" someone shouted and ran to Coyote and struck him dead. And again, much later, no one remembered who or what struck the blow which killed Coyote for the second time.

Then from the left hand side of center, Coyote ran out swinging a great club and struck at his fallen selves until all that remained were two masses of fur and blood and broken bones and twisted sinew.

Then Coyote danced the dance of victory over his own fallen selves, pledging their death to his own great anger. Oh, he danced, he really danced.

Now then," said Porcupine, "how is it that this one who dances the victory in battle dance, when it was not himself who killed himselves? Is it within reason for him to claim this doubtful victory?"

"If I did not kill these two, then who did kill them?" demanded Coyote. "Let him step forward to claim these deaths, that I may kill him too in revenge."

When no one stepped forward, Coyote declared, motioning to his dead selves, "Then obviously, these kills are mine!"

"It seems to me," began Elk, who was interrupted by Skunk who also began, "It's quite obvious to me that. . . ."

"Now hold on a moment," said Badger.

And Coyote wheeled on Badger, shouting, "Hah! Don't you know that you can't hold onto a moment, let alone a minute?"

And so they argued, all the animal creatures, about the finer points of who might or might not claim a kill.

And the women of these brave warriors, at the urging of Coyote, prepared a great feast so that these mighty warrior-debators might continue on full stomachs.

And soon, the recent anger was set aside for the more important battle of words leading to reason.

And by this time, everyone having forgotten all about Coyote, he, Coyote, took his fallen selves by their tails and dragged them away uphill.

Then he took a good hot sweat bath and then sang a song of renewal known only to himself, and soon his other selves revived.

"Now," said one of them, "that's what I'd call making your point the hard way. You know, it really hurt when you killed me."

"Yes," said the other self, standing up and stretching, "the next time this happens, don't forget it'll be your turn to be killed."

"Hey, maybe this won't ever happen again, huh?"

"Oh, it will happen again," Coyote said. "Yes, it always seems to happen again."

Then he merged into himselves and walked away, far away.

—A COYOTE STORY BY NATIVE AMERICAN AUTHOR PETER BLUE CLOUD

Ta shih hua hsiao,
hsiao shih hua wu.

Convert great quarrels into small ones,
and small ones into nothing.

—A CHINESE PROVERB

The Rose Prince 🌿

O nce upon a time, a rose bush grew at the edge of a forest. The bush had beautiful roses; each blossom was more splendid than the last. One day, the bush produced a bud lovelier than all the others. The bud was so large and heavy that the bush bent to the ground. When the bud opened, there was a human child inside. The rose had given birth to a son.

The Queen of the country was walking near the rim of the forest. Queen Rhoda heard a baby's cry. She followed the sound to the rose bush and found the fragrant child lying on the petals. The Queen wrapped the baby in her purple veil and carried him back to the palace.

Several weeks later King Laurin returned from battle. He found the Queen in her rose bower. She was swinging a wicker cradle hung from satin ribbons. The King saw the infant inside the cradle and smiled. King Laurin and Queen Rhoda accepted the child as their own.

They were childless and the Queen was long past childbearing age. Once the palace had been filled with the laughter of seven sons. But one by one the laughing voices were stilled as each prince was slain in the ceaseless battle that raged across the country. The reason for the war was lost in memory because it was so ancient. But now King Laurin fought to avenge the deaths of his seven sons.

The Rose Prince grew in strength and grace. The King taught him to ride horseback and to swordfight. The Queen taught him to play his lute and to write poetry. His happiest moments were spent in the Queen's rose bower and in the forest.

As the Prince reached manhood, he was to be knighted. On the eve of the ceremony, he sat alone in the chapel and watched over his armor. The Queen came and sat with him in the candlelight. She told him of his birth and the rose bush who was his mother.

During the pink dawn, the Prince knelt before the King and pledged to right the ancient wrongs. He kissed the Queen farewell and rode to battle by the King's side. By the time the sun was overhead, the Prince was on a battlefield surrounded by the sound of screams and the smell of blood. He saw the King cut from his horse and run through with a lance. He heard the dying King call to him to avenge his death. He felt the anger burn in his brain. He reared his horse and pursued the King's slayer towards the forest. The Prince knocked the man from his horse and cut the lance from his hand.

As he lifted his sword to strike again, he saw the wild roses under the pines. There was blood on the roses. In an instant, he felt the hatred that clouded his brain. He loathed the murderous intent of his heart. The Prince told the soldier, "Flee—while I am still in my right mind." The soldier ran; the Prince was alone in the serenity of the forest. He vowed to end the carnage.

The Rose Prince returned to the battlefield. He gathered the fallen banners of all the countries and held them high over his head. "Stop the battle," his voice rang out. One by one, the soldiers stopped fighting. The battle ceased. The Prince spoke softly of surrender and reconciliation. His message was of love and sweetness. The soldiers began to cast off their armor and weapons. One by one, each turned and went home.

The Prince walked to the forest. He called out, "I am of you. Where is the rose bush that bore the splendid blossoms?"

A nightingale replied, "She is dead. She was a noble tree and had a prince for a flower."

"I am that prince. The juice of the rose still runs in my veins. I wish to return to a life of fragrance and beauty. I wish to leave this human life."

The nightingale said, "Dear Prince, I will stay with you and sing your soul back to a rose."

The Prince knelt on the spot where he was born. At nightfall, the nightingale began to sing. The melody cast out all memory of the world of men. The Prince sank into the moss and loam; his limbs took root in the earth. By dawn, a tall and thornless rose tree had bloomed. And for as long as the rose tree lived, there was peace in the land.

—A TALE FROM ROMANIA, RETOLD BY SHARON CREEDON

La gracia no es vivir,
la gracia es saber vivir.

The blessing is not in living,
but in knowing how to live.

—A MEXICAN-AMERICAN
PROVERB

THE NEVER-ENDING WORK

A Legend of Avalokitesvara ❧

The Bodhisattva Avalokitesvara looked down into the many hells and saw that they were filled with suffering beings.

A great vow spontaneously arose in his heart. "I will liberate all beings from the sufferings of the hells," he said. And so through countless ages he labored, descending into and emptying hell after hell, until the unimaginable task was at last done.

The great Bodhisattva ceased then from his eons of heroic exertion. He wiped the glistening diamonds of beaded sweat from his brow, and, looking down into the now empty hells, smiled. It was done. Here and there a curling wisp of smoke still rose up. Now and then, in some vast cavern far below, faint echoes sounded as a loose brick shifted on a pile of rubble. But the raging fires had been quenched and the great iron cauldrons were quiet. Sweet silence flowed through the dark halls. Even the demons were gone for they too, in the end, had been released, liberated to the heavens, by the mighty efforts of the Compassionate One.

But what was this? Suddenly, there came a wailing scream, then another, and another. Flames leapt, clouds of smoke whirled, blood-filled cauldrons bubbled madly. The radiant smile faded from the Bodhisattva's face. Once again the hells were entirely filled. In less than an instant all was exactly as before.

The heart of the Bodhisattva Avalokitesvara filled with sorrow. Suddenly, his head split into many heads. His arms shattered into many arms. The one thousand heads looked in all directions to see the sufferings of every being. The one thousand arms were enough to reach into any realm, to save those in need.

Rolling up his one thousand sleeves, the great Bodhisattva settled down once more to the unending task.

—A TALE FROM INDIA, RETOLD BY RAFE MARTIN

Puu ei katu yhellä lyöntilla.

A tree does not fall with one blow.

—A FINNISH PROVERB

CHOICES

Holding Up the Sky

One day an elephant saw a hummingbird lying
flat on its back on the ground.
The bird's tiny feet were raised up into the air.

"What on earth are you doing, Hummingbird?"
asked the elephant.

The hummingbird replied,
"I have heard that the sky might fall today.
If that should happen,
I am ready to do my bit in holding it up."

The elephant laughed and mocked the tiny bird.
"Do you think THOSE little feet could hold up the SKY?"

"Not alone," admitted the hummingbird.
"But each must do what he can.
And this is what *I* can do."

—A TALE FROM CHINA

ॐ

E waikahi ka pono i manalo.

It is well to be united in thought,
that all men have peace.

—A HAWAIIAN PROVERB

A NOTE TO STORYTELLERS
AND DISCUSSION LEADERS

Wondering what our folk wisdom had to say about peace, I began looking for folktales on themes of peace. Not suprisingly, self-protection and one-upsmanship are more popular folktale themes than are cooperation and peaceful co-existence. However, I did find several interesting tales which may help you to think about the possibility of peace.

These tales were selected in the hope that they will give the reader pause for thought. A few are designed for use in storytelling, others might best be shared through reading aloud or through silent reading. All should lend themselves to discussion, though there are times when a story is most effective if left to settle into the listener's thoughts on its own.

When I asked other storytellers for peace story suggestions they almost always mentioned Bill Harley's "Freedom Bird" story right away. That is the story of a bird who cannot be killed and escapes the hunter. The bird really does nothing to bring about peace—he simply escapes with his freedom, while taunting the hunter. It is curious that so many folks think freedom and peace are the same thing. In fact, they are probably not compatible concepts. To achieve peace we must give up some freedoms. The essence of peaceful co-existence probably still lies in the old adage, "Your right to swing your elbow ends where your neighbor's elbow begins."

In seeking material for this book I looked for tales which showed a way to achieve peace. Facile stories suggesting that we all simply join hands and love each other did not interest me, nor did the many stories of peace achieved through the winning of wars. Peace requires constant mainte-nance. It is hard work. A never-ending task.

Storyteller Marcia Lane in her paper, "Stories: The Voice of Peace: An Agenda for Peace and Creative Problem-Solving," makes some excellent suggestions for us all in the following passage:

It is . . . no more useful to tell a child to "think peaceful thoughts"
than it is to tell him/her to fly! So how can we promote inner

harmony and, eventually and inevitably, harmony between people? By using stories to do three things:

- To encourage children to look inward.
- To present kids with several possible answers to a problem.
- To give children a positive sense of value and purpose—a sense of their own strength and inherent morality.

Most of us have stories in our repertoire that can accomplish these goals. We need to identify those stories, songs, poems, games which work in subtle ways to encourage creative problem-solving. . . . Try to look at your existing materials with an eye/ear to whether they send positive messages, give alternatives to violence, recognize and reject prejudice, and applaud cooperation and collaboration.

One last thought: When we try to tell "peace stories" by eviscerating traditional myths and folktales, we end up with dishonest storytelling, and the inevitable sense that the teller imagines a world without adventure, danger, variety, or disagreement. It is probably undesirable (and certainly impossible!) to eliminate conflict in the world. But it is possible, through the stories we tell and the ways in which we discuss them, to expand the choices for living in harmony.

In studying the world's folktales I have come to the conclusion that these tales present a mirror of the mind of mankind. Throughout history, and wherever humans reside on this planet, their tales speak repeatedly of the same concerns, and reach similar conclusions. In the past mankind's tales have stressed trickery and power more often than conflict resolution. Is it possible that by changing the tales we tell we can change our warring nature? It is worth a try.

RECOMMENDED BOOKS
ABOUT PEACE
FOR CHILDREN AND ADULTS

To Help Kids Think About the Possibilities of Peace:

The Big Book of Peace edited by Ann Durrell and Marilyn Sachs. New York: Dutton, 1990.

The Fragile Flag by Jane Langton. New York: Harper & Row, 1984. A children's crusade to stop missile making.

"Grandfather Bear Is Hungry" in *Look Back and See: Lively Tales for Gentle Tellers* by Margaret Read MacDonald. New York: H. W. Wilson, 1991. Chipmunk's sharing calms an irate bear.

"Hug 'o War" in *Where the Sidewalk Ends* by Shel Silverstein. New York: Harper & Row, 1974. A fun poem to speak or act out.

Irene-Peace: Includes a Play/ Aristophanes by Sofia Zarambouka. Washington, D.C.: Tee Loftin, 1979. A picture book based on Aristophanes' play "Peace." Includes a playlet for kids to perform.

My Love You, My Children: 101 Stories for Children of All Ages by M. R. Bawa Muhaiyadeen. Philadelphia: The Fellowship Press, 1981. Strange and lovely moral tales for children by a Sufi master of Sri Lanka.

My World Peace: Thought and Illustrations from the Children of All Nations by Richard Exley and Helen Exley. Lincolnwood, Ill.: Passport Books, 1985. Letters and thoughts from children around the world.

Peace Begins With You by Katherine Scholes. Illus. by Robert Ingpen. San Francisco: Sierra Club/Little, Brown 1989. A gentle discussion of the choices that bring about peace, in picture book format.

Tistou of the Green Thumbs by Maurice Druon. New York: Charles Scribner's Sons, 1958. Plants grow wherever Tistou places his hands. He places them on his father's armaments factory.

The Wheel of King Asoka by Ashok Davar. Chicago: Follett, 1977. True story of this Indian ruler who abandoned war for peace. Pillars inscribed with his philosophy still stand throughout India.

A Select List for Adults Who Work with Kids:

. . . And the Earth Lived Happily Every After: Old and New Traditional Tales to Wage Peace edited by Floating Eagle Feather. Metairie, La: Wages of Peace, 1987.

"Children and War" by Norma Law. Position paper for the Association of Childhood Education International. February 1973. A survey of research on children's attitudes toward war. Send 35 cents to: Association for Childhood Education International, 3615 Wisconsin Ave. N.W., Washington, D.C., 20016.

Helping Young Children Understand Peace, War, and the Nuclear Threat by Nancy Carlsson-Paige and Diane E. Levin. Washington, D.C.: National Association for the Education of Young Children, 1985.

Learning the Skills of Peacemaking: An Activity Guide for Elementary-Age Children on Communication, Cooperating, Resolving Conflict by Naomi Drew. Rolling Hills Estates, Calif.: Jalmar Press, 1987. (Write to: 145 Hitching Post Drive, Building 2, Rolling Hills Estates, Calif. 90274).

Weaving Words, Spinning Hope: A Collection of Stories and Teacher Activities to Help Children Explore Issues of Peace, Justice, and Social Awareness compiled by Storytellers for World Change Network. Philadelphia: New Society Press, 1991.

TALE NOTES WITH SOME SUGGESTIONS FOR STORYTELLING AND PROVERB SOURCES

Motifs given are from Stith Thompson, *Motif-Index of Folk-Literature* (Bloomington, Ind.: Indiana University Press, 1955), and Margaret Read MacDonald, *The Storyteller's Sourcebook: A Subject, Title, and Motif Index to Folklore Collections for Children.* (Detroit: Gale/Neal-Schuman, 1982).

Page 1: "The Gates of Paradise" in *Zen Flesh, Zen Bones: A Collection of Zen and Pre-Zen Writings* by Paul Reps. (Rutland, Vt.: Charles Tuttle, 1957), p. 51–52.

Page 5: "Two Goats on the Bridge" is retold by Margaret Read MacDonald. A brief variant of this tale appears in *Three Rolls and One Doughnut: Fables from Russia* by Mirra Ginsburg. Illus. by Anita Lobel. (New York: Dial Press, 1970).

   Type 202, Motif W167.1 *Two stubborn goats meet each other on a bridge. The Types of the Folktale* (Helsinki: Folklore Fellows Communications, 1973) cites variants of this tale from Germany, Livonia, and Turkey.

Page 7: "The Neighbor's Shifty Son" is retold by Margaret Read MacDonald from a Chinese folktale. A brief variant appears in *Tales from Old China* by Isabelle Chang (New York: Random, 1948), p.52.

Page 8: "A Dervish Hosts the Mullah" is an Iranian tale retold by Margaret Read MacDonald. An excellent version of this tale appears in *The Exploits of the Incomparable Mullah Nasrudin* by Idries Shah (New York: Simon and Schuster, 1966), p. 60–62.

Page 10: "Reaching for the Moon" is retold by Margaret Read MacDonald. A variant of this tale is found as "The Monkeys and the Moon" in *Tibetan Folk Tales* by Frederick and Audry Hyde-Chambers (Boston: Shambhala, 1981), p. 96

   You may want to compare this tale to Motif J1791.2 *Rescuing the Moon* and Motif J2133.5 *Men hang down in a chain until top man spits on his hands.*

Page 12: "Strength" is retold by Margaret Read MacDonald. A fine variant of this tale appears in *Limba Stories and Storytelling* by Ruth Finegan (Oxford: Clarendon, 1967).

Suggestions for telling: This retelling is easy to learn and powerful when told. Here are a few hints for the telling. The audience may enjoy joining in on the animals' chorus, "Strength! Strength! Strength! Strength!" and the story can be developed as a lively participation event. However, though this story is energetic and humorous in its telling, the ending must be delivered in a serious manner, cutting directly across the audience's excited mood and expectations. Practice the ending carefully before attempting it, so that you are certain you can carry the audience through the tale's abrupt mood change at its end. Children often buy into Man's "triumph" at the tale's end, and are brought up short when they realize that his actions were perhaps not a triumph after all. This powerful story is one that children need to hear.

Page 18: "Not Our Problem" is retold by Margaret Read MacDonald. Variants may be found in *Burmese and Thai Fairy Tales* by Eleanor Brockett (Chicago: Follett, 1965), p. 150–152; *A Kingdom for a Drop of Honey and Other Burmese Folktales* by Maung Htin Aung and Helen G. Trager (New York: Parents' Magazine Press, 1969), p. 29–30; and in *Tales from Thailand* by Marian Davies Toth (Rutland, Vt.: Charles Tuttle, 1971), p. 40–48.

Motif N381, *Drop of honey causes chain of accidents*, is a much used motif, with both European and Asian variants.

Suggestions for telling: Children may want to join you on the refrain "It's not *our* problem," though this is a quiet, thoughtful story rather than a rowdy "audience participation" tale.

Page 21: "A Man With No Brain" is from the repertoire of Mohammed Bel-Halfaoui, translated and contributed by Cathryn Wellner of Duncan, British Columbia. Cathryn writes: "I learned the story in Paris during my first visit with the ebullient Mohammed Bel-Halfaoui. He had invited several storytellers for an evening of couscous and tale telling. . . . Wine flowed freely, along with steaming plates of couscous. The stories began before the first bite and continued long into the night. "A Man With No Brain" was among them. Mohammed Bel-Halfaoui told us he had heard the stories at the knee of his mother, Zohar. In Arabic they were melodic, rhythmic. They lost some of their poetry in French but retained their vigor and underlying lessons. Mohammed danced around the room as he told them, eyes snapping, arms waving.

"Mohammed is a retired professor of Arabic, who taught in Germany and France and finally retired to Paris. It was not until he retired and happened upon a storytelling event that he realized that the stories of his childhood might be interesting to someone else. Now he jumps at every chance to share them. He would be pleased to have one of them included in a book of stories for peace."

Page 23: "The Weapon" is based on "The Sun, His Myth" in *Kathlamet Texts*, edited by Franz Boas. Smithsonian Institution, Bureau of American Ethnology, Bulletin 26. (Washington, D.C.: Government Printing Office, 1901), p. 26–33. This story was told in 1891 by Charles Cultee of Bay Center, Washington, who had formerly lived at Cathlamet, Oregon on the Columbia River. This retelling by Margaret Read MacDonald is based on Boas's word-by-word transliteration of the Kathlamet text, rather than on Boas's own retelling.

Suggestions for telling: This lengthy and dark tale is more difficult to learn than most, but is worth the effort. Its building horror will engross your audience, and its consistent repetition will help you keep your place in the tale, despite its length. I have paced my retelling directly on the Kathlamet teller's text.

Page 32: "The Ass's Shadow" from *The Storyteller's Calendar: 1991* by Ruth Stotter (Stinson Beach, Calif.: Stotter Press, 1991).

See Motif J1169.7 *Suit about the ass's shadow.* A familiar Aesop's fable.

Page 33: "The Snipe and the Mussel" from Peng Tong, *Warring States Anecdotes*, compiled by Liu Xang, as quoted in ". . . And the Earth Lived Happily Ever After": Old and New Traditional Tales to Wage Peace* edited by Floating Eagle Feather. (Metairie, La.: Wages of Peace, 1987).

Motif J219.1 *Enemies lose lives to a third party rather than make peace.* Chinese variants also appear in *Tales from Old China* by Isabelle Chang (New York, Random, 1948), p. 46–47 (clam and crane fight), and in *Tricky Peik and Other Picture Tales* by Jeanne Hardendorff (Philadelphia: Lippincott, 1967), p. 41–43 (oyster and heron fight).

Page 34: "Fighting Leads to Losses," a Jataka story from India, is retold by Cathy Spagnoli in " . . . And the Earth Lived Happily Ever After."

Motif K452.1.2 *Fox divides fish for two others. Head to one, tail to other, middle for fox.* This Jataka tale appears in *The Fables of India* by

Joseph Gaer (Boston: Little, Brown, 1955), p. 139–141, and *The Talking Beasts: Myths, Fables and Poems of India* by Gwendolyn Reed (New York: Lothrop, Lee, and Shepard, 1969), p. 62–63. A monkey tricks cats in a Japanese variant in *The Sea of Gold and Other Tales from Japan* by Yoshiko Uchida (New York: Scribner's, 1965), p. 55–60, and a fox tricks bears in a Hungarian version, *Two Greedy Bears* by Mirra Ginsburg (New York: Macmillan, 1976).

Page 35: "How the Short-ears Conquered the Long-ears" in *Legends of the South Seas* by Anthony Alpers (New York: Thomas Y. Crowell, 1970), p. 247–250.

Page 39: "The War Between the Sandpipers and the Whales" is retold by Margaret Read MacDonald. Variants of this tale may be found in *Legends of the South Seas, Book I* by Eve Grey (Honolulu: Island Import Company, 1954) as "The Whale and the Sandpiper," p. 23–27 and in *The Magic Calabash* by Jean Cothran (New York: David McKay, 1954), as "Coral Sea Contest," p. 38–45.

Grey says of this tale: "The story of the whale and the sandpiper was a favorite sleep-time chant in the Marshall Islands. It was sung about many birds and many fish. The chants of the whale and the sandpiper were sung each time a new fish or bird was named." Grey tells us that the grandfather or grandmother would take the youngest children aside while the others visited around the bonfire. Laying down with the little ones on a mat, the grandmother or grandfather would tell a story such as this, chanting it on and on until every child was asleep. "No child ever heard the story to the end. First the youngest went to sleep, then the others, one by one. Their father or grandfather carried them inside the house and put them down upon sleeping mats." Next evening the children would ask what happened, and the grandparent would start the story all over again.

Suggestions for telling: This tale has been retold for audience participation telling. Children will love joining you on the chants of whale and sandpiper. It is fun also to let the audience provide names of the sandpiper cousins and the whale cousins which will be called. I pause the story for quite a while at these points, letting many children suggest names of seabirds and sea creatures. At the tale's end, children love to munch with the whales and drink up the sea—"Sluuurp!"— with the sandpipers. And of course they delight in spitting it all back!

If my audience is familiar with the concept of "habitat" I sometimes let the sandpipers and whales comment at the end, "We're destroying our own *habitats!*" In addition to its clear message about the total devastation caused by war, this tale will be useful to those wanting stories on ecological themes.

Page 48: "The Black Hound" in *The Hungry Tigress* by Rafe Martin (Berkeley, Calif.: Parallax Press, 1990), p. 128–129. This is a retelling of a legend from India. In Martin's discussion of the tale in *The Hungry Tigress* he compares the terror caused by the Black Hound to that caused by the threat of nuclear war.

Page 53: "Two Goats on the Bridge" is retold by Margaret Read MacDonald from Motif J133.1 *One wild goat steps over another. They thus pass each other uninjured on a cliff. This shows advantage of peaceableness.*

Page 55: "How Friendship Began Among Birds" in *Burmese Folk Tales* by Maung Htin Aung (New Delhi: Oxford University Press, 1948), p. 50–51.

Page 57: "The Lion's Whisker" in *The Lion's Whisker: Tales of High Africa* by Brent Ashabranner and Russell Davis (Boston: Little, Brown, 1959), p. 7–9. This is a Somali variant from Ethiopia.

   Motif B848.21 *Woman removes lion's whisker without harm to self.* An Amhara variant appears in *African Village Folktales* by Edna Mason Kaula (New York: World, 1968), p. 142–145. A Korean variant is found in *The Tiger's Whisker* by Harold Courlander (New York: Harcourt, Brace, and World, 1957), p. 16–19.

Page 60: "Temper" in *Zen Flesh, Zen Bones*, p. 101.

Page 61: "The Advice of Hatim al-Asamm" is retold by Margaret Read MacDonald. Mention of this tale appears in *Learning How to Learn: Psychology and Spirituality in the Sufi Way* by Idries Shah (San Francisco: Harper & Row, 1978), p. 152.

Page 62: "Music to Soothe the Savage Breast" in *Japanese Tales* edited and translated by Royall Tyler (New York: Pantheon, 1987), p. 93.

Page 63: "Slops" is retold by Margaret Read MacDonald. Variants may be found in *Welsh Legendary Tales* by Elisabeth Sheppard-Jones (Edinburgh: Thomas Nelson, 1959), p. 156–158 and in *Fairy Tales from the British Isles* by Amabel Williams-Ellis (New York: Frederick Warne, 1960), p. 76–81.

   Suggestions for telling: Preschool or primary children will enjoy peeling the potatoes, carrots, and onions with you, and tossing the peelings into the "slop bucket." We all end up saying "slop bucket" together. Then let them hoist the heavy bucket and grunt as the old man crosses the floor, "Unh . . . unh . . . unh . . . unh . . . ," and goes out the door. We all count the steps aloud together as we struggle with our heavy weight: "One, two, three, four, five, six, seven, eight, nine, TEN . . . *SLOSH!*"

Page 69: "Nansen Cuts the Cat in Two" in *Zen Flesh, Zen Bones*, p.101.

Page 70: "A Lesson for Kings" in *Indian Folk and Fairy Tales* by Joseph Jacobs (New York: Putnam, n.d.), p. 155–159.

Page 72: "Heaven and Hell" is retold by Margaret Read MacDonald. Motif W47.1 *Cooperation: Everyone in hell has to use yard-long chopsticks.* Variants of this appear in *Tales from Old China* by Isabelle Chang, p.47–49 and *Stories to Solve* by George Shannon (New York: Greenwillow, 1985), p. 51–53.

Western storytellers have developed a variant in which the diner's arms are formed without elbows, making it impossible to bring a fork to the mouth. A version of this appears in *Stories for Telling: A Treasury for Christian Storytellers* by William P. White (Minneapolis: Augsburg, 1986), p. 70.

Page 73: "A Blind Man Catches a Bird" in *Children of Wax: African Folk Tales* by Alexander McCall Smith (New York: Interlink Books, 1989), p. 58–60.

Page 76: "Old Joe and the Carpenter" by Pleasant DeSpain. Pleasant De-Spain kindly gave permission for inclusion of his story in this book. He writes: "Old Joe has become my 'signature story' over these years. . . . It has been reprinted in several magazines and IBM/*Good Housekeeping Magazine* have sent it to every elementary school in the U.S. Many, many storytellers have asked my permission to tell it, and I have usually given same with the understanding that it remains my tale and that I'm given credit each time told. . . . I heard the bare bones of the tale from an elementary librarian many years past during one of my school tours. She heard it from her father. I believe it is an authentic American folktale, and I've had the good fortune to flesh it out and bring it back into the oral tradition. . . . The tale embodies the essence of my storytelling philosophy: Bridges unify. And we always have the choice to build or destroy with our words and actions."

This tale strikes me as an authored piece, rather than a folktale, but certainly Pleasant's widespread distribution of the tale has brought it into use by storytellers throughout the U.S. Many have heard him tell this and have added the story to their own repertoires.

Page 79: "Two Foxes" in *Folk Stories of the South* by M.A. Jagendorf (New York: Vanguard Press, 1972), p. 306–308.

Page 82: "Lifting the Sky" is a transcription of Vi Hilbert's telling during a workshop at the University of Hawaii Hilo, in 1991. Vi's written version of this story appears as "Yehaw!" in *Huboo: Lushooteed Literature in English* by Vi Hilbert (Vi (Taqʷšeblu) Hilbert, 1980), p. 131–133. Vi writes: "William Shelton told this story to audiences in the Marysville, Everett area [of Washington state] where he lived. He wanted all children to know about the lessons imbedded within it. He would be happy to have it reach a wider audience I am sure."

Suggestions for telling: When Vi tells this story she asks the audience members to each find a long pole and help her lift the sky. As they shoulder their pretend poles and push upward, Vi encourages them to keep trying harder. Laughing, she tells them that they are not pushing hard enough, and she admonishes them to try again . . ."This time push HARD!" At last, all calling "YeHAW!" together, the group succeeds in lifting the sky. Vi wishes this story to be shared through reading or telling. Rights for commercial use, however, reside with the Lushootseed Research Center.

Page 86: Peacemaking Technique #1: "Halving the Cookie" is contributed by Margaret Read MacDonald. This is a widely used American folk tradition.

Page 87: Peacemaking Technique #2: "The Argument Sticks" is retold by Margaret Read MacDonald from "How Two Indian Boys Settled a Quarrel" in *Stories the Iroquois Tell Their Children* by Mabel Powers (New York: American Book Company, 1917), p. 125–129.

Page 88: Peacemaking Technique #3: "Looking Your Enemy in the Eye" is contributed from the family tradition of Jennifer Sorenson, Hamden, Connecticut.

Page 89: "Buddha Prevents a War" in *Myths of the Hindus & Buddhists* by Ananda K. Coomaraswamy and Sister Nivedita (New York: Dover, 1967), p. 278.

Page 91: "The Battle" in *Elderberry Flute Song* by Peter Blue Cloud. (Trumansburg, New York: Crossing Press, 1982), p. 64–66.

Page 94: "The Rose Prince" retold by Sharon Creedon. © Sharon Creedon, 1991. This is based on a Romanian folktale in *Myths and Legends of Flowers, Trees, Fruits and Plants* by Charles Skinner (Philadelphia: J.B. Lippincott, 1911).

Page 97: "The Legend of Avalokitesvara" in *The Hungry Tigress* by Rafe Martin, p. 64.

Page 99: "Holding Up the Sky" is retold by Margaret Read MacDonald. A variant appears in *Tales from Old China* by Isabelle Chang, p. 9–10.

Proverb Sources:

A Collection of Chinese Proverbs by Rev. W. Scarborough. Revised and enlarged by Rev. C. Wilfrid Allan (New York: Paragon, 1964).

A Dictionary of Mexican-American Proverbs compiled by Mark Glazer (New York: Greenwood Press, 1987).

Finnish Proverbs translated by Inkeri Vaananen-Jensen (Iowa City, Iowa: Penfield Press, 1990).

German Proverbs by Edmund P. Kremer (Stanford, Calif.: Stanford University Press, 1955).

Japanese Proverbs and Sayings by Daniel Crump Buchanan (Norman, Okla: University of Oklahoma, 1965).

Malay Proverbs by Sir John Winstedt (London: John Murray, 1950).

Mexican-American Folklore by John O. West (Little Rock, Ark.: August House, 1988).

'Olelo No'eau: Hawaiian Proverbs & Poetical Sayings by Mary Kawena Pukui (Honolulu, Hi.: Bishop Museum Press, 1983).

Persian Proverbs by L. P. Elwell-Sutton (London: John Murray, 1859).

Scandinavian Proverbs by Julie Jensen McDonald (Iowa City, Iowa: Penfield Press, 1985).

Türk ata Sözleri by M. N. Özön (Istanbul: 1952).

A World of Proverbs by Patricia Houghton (Poole, Dorset, England: Blandford Press, 1981).

A World Treasury of Proverbs from Twenty-Five Languages by Henry Davidoff (New York: Random House, 1946).

ACKNOWLEDGMENTS

"The Ass's Shadow," an Aesop fable from *A Story Teller's Calendar for 1991*. Compiled by Ruth Stotter. Stotter Press, 1990. Permission of Ruth Stotter.

"The Battle" from *Elderberry Flute Song* by Peter Blue Cloud. Fredonia, NY: White Pine Press, 1982. Permission of White Pine Press.

"The Black Hound" and "A Legend of Avalokitesvara" in *The Hungry Tigress* by Rafe Martin, Berkeley: Parallax Press, © 1990. Permission of Parallax Press and the author.

"A Blind Man Catches a Bird" from *Children of Wax* by Alexander McCall Smith. New York: Interlink Books, 1990. © 1990 Alexander McCall Smith. Permission of Interlink Books.

"Buddha Prevents a War" from *Myths of the Hindus and Buddhists* by Ananda K. Coomaraswamy and Sister Nivedita. New York: Dover, 1967. Permission of Dover Publications, Inc.

"Lifting the Sky" is from "The Changer" in *Huboo: Lushootseed Literature in English* by Vi (Taqʷšeblu) Hilbert, © 1980. Permission granted by Lushootseed Research. Altered to match Vi Hilbert's oral retelling with permission of Vi (Taqʷšeblu) Hilbert.

"Fighting Leads to Losses" by Cathy Spagnoli from *. . . And the Earth Lived Happily Ever After: Old and New Traditional Tales to Wage Peace* edited by Floating Eagle Feather. Metairie, La: Wages of Peace, 1987. Permission of Cathy Spagnoli.

"The Gates of Paradise," "Nansen Cuts the Cat in Two," and "Temper" from *Zen Flesh, Zen Bones* by Paul Reps, Rutland, Vt.: Charles E. Tuttle Co., Inc. © 1957. Permission of Charles E. Tuttle Co., Inc.

"How Friendship Began Among Birds" from *Burmese Folk Tales* by Maung Htin Aung. London: Oxford University Press, 1948. Permission of Oxford University Press.

"How the Short-ears Conquered the Long-ears." Excerpts from *Legends of the South Seas* by Anthony Alpers. © 1970 by Anthony Alpers. Reprinted by permission of HarperCollins Publishers.

"The Lion's Whisker" from *The Lion's Whisker* by Russell G. Davis and Brent K. Ashabranner. Boston: Little, Brown, 1959. © 1959 and 1987 by Russell G. Davis and Brent K. Ashabranner. Reprinted by permission of the authors.

"Old Joe and the Carpenter" by Pleasant DeSpain. All rights held by author. Permission of Pleasant DeSpain.

"The Rose Prince" by Sharon Creedon. Unpublished story. © 1987 by Sharon Creedon. Permission of Sharon Creedon.

"Music to Soothe the Savage Breast" from *Japanese Tales* by Royall Tyler. © 1987 by Royall Tyler. Reprinted by permission of Pantheon Books, a division of Random House, Inc.

"Two Foxes" from *Folk Stories of the South* by M.A. Jagendorf. © 1972, 1973 by Vanguard Press. Reprinted by permission of Vanguard Press, a division of Random House, Inc..

Thank You

To all the Seattle Storytellers' Guild members who suggested peace tales, but particularly to Lynn Kohner and to Naomi Baltuck who suggested many tales. And to Sharon Creedon, Pleasant DeSpain, Vi Hilbert, Cathy Spagnoli, and Cathryn Wellner, for sharing tales from their own repertoires.

To Doug Bland, Jon Porcino, and Nancy Schimmel for sharing their bibliographies of peace tales and to Marcia Lane for permission to reprint her very cogent comments about using folktales on themes of peace.

To Carlton Appelo, Dr. Ilhan Basgöz, Gloria Durán, Dr. Alain Gowing, Eleanora Hillis, Winifred Jaegger, Ben Wirkkala, and Parveen Zadeh for help in translating proverbs.

To Jennifer MacDonald for typing this manuscript, and to Diantha Thorpe and Jim Thorpe of Shoe String for believing in this project enough to publish it.

And most especially to Diantha for spending hours of editorial cogitation making sure this book speaks clearly for the possibilities of peaceful resolution.

MULTICULTURAL INDEX